The Translator

The Translator

A Novel by
Pat Goodheart

VanVactor & Goodheart
Cambridge, Massachusetts

Published in 1983 by
Van Vactor & Goodheart, Inc.
24 Lee Street
Cambridge, Massachusetts 02139

The Translator was originally published clothbound by Holt, Rinehart and Winston in 1979.

Library of Congress Cataloging in Publication Data

Goodheart, Pat.
The translator.
I. Title.
PS3557.0582T7 1983   813'.54   83-14542
ISBN 0-941324-07-9 (pbk.)

Printed in the United States of America

The Translator

1

Femme de Ménage

Madame Propre comes to me at eight forty-five, not a minute later, and try as I do, I cannot wake up without the turn of the key in the lock. She comes to me five days and worries how I manage the other two. And she is right. When she isn't here, I dream of the key turning in the lock. The days are not the same and I awake with the sense of feeling guilty at a quarter to twelve. Sleeping fretfully through her time, I awake exhausted. . . . The rest of the day, I try to recover lost hours.

Monday. . . . As a new mother awaits her baby's first cry, so I await the turn of the key in the lock. How she rouses me from this bed! I rush to the shower. In and out. Bonjour, Madame! Yes, I'll have my coffee now. Won't you sit down? I am mad to ask. She never will. I don't know why I ask. . . . Madame Propre notices I bought the coffee in the prisunic. Yes, it is cheaper than in the épicerie. I know. How could I help but know? She's told me before. And I give her my answer like a catechism. How she shouts in my ear! She shouts in my ear because I'm American. I'll always be American to Madame. I couldn't really understand, and so she shouts.

Madame sees my new skirt. "Combien ça coûte?" she wants to know. I'll tell her, as it is our bond. The cost of living is high. "Ça coûte cher. Cent cinquante francs." "Ça m'étonne pas. Mais voyons comment elle est faite!" Together, we examine the hand-finished hem and the silk lining. She is all patience with me. I am the ingenue. I must be taught that she is mistress of my world.

Madame Propre is very well informed, better than myself. She reads the papers. "Le ministre chez vous était assassiné ce matin." Who can she mean? "Au Canada." All things and persons North and South American are mine. The riots in the ghettos have to do with me. My houses are vandalized. All fires reflect the moral imperfection in which I exist. I am the rich and the poor. This is my America and she will not let me forget it. So it is I drink America in the morning with Madame's talk.

I read *Le Monde*. Madame is right. Someone was assassinated in Canada this morning. The French and the pro-English are at it again. Secession's in the air, a deputy is dead. I doubt they'll carry it through. They only want to make a show of it.

I need not search for my America. We make good

copy here, and though my eye would resist, I am led by her talk to the headlines. But why so much of the Russians and the Italians? This is not what I would read. Ah, here we are sending more aid to Southeast Asia. Which is it, Cambodia or Vietnam? What are they doing with so many advisers? Do they listen to them or are they on their own, planning a strategy? When she leaves the room, I think I'll turn to the back of the paper.

For some people, it is soap operas, for others, it is popular songs. For me, it is the want ads. I glance quickly through things for sale to find the treasure which is never there: through property, apartments for rent or sale, hectares in Auvergne or Brittany. There is still time. It is not too late to buy. I dally between the mountains and the sea. I dream of the sea without people but find myself price-wise in economically depressed mountain regions. I have a liking for a landscape which is grand. I do not like bumps, I like hills and vistas. They inspire me. I think of the history of man, I think of my own history. . . . It is always the same. Madame's at my shoulder again. The coffee is cold. Should she pour a fresh cup? She should. "Il y a des familles qui dépensent tout leur argent comme ça! C'est pas bon." Madame shakes her head. I must acknowledge my guilt. It is better that way. I will see then how I am wasteful and she prudent, that with my cold coffee and my cigarettes, I am drinking and smoking away my advantages, my house in the country, an education for my unborn children.

Another kidnapping! Thirty Basques are wanted in

exchange for an aging cabinet member. I hope they come to terms. Though I do not like the idea of bargaining with such people, I prefer it to murder. I think of what happened in Belgium. They took an embassy official, I think. Was he Israeli? I no longer remember.

Often, the violence is on my side. But today, at least, we are even. With the drop in the lira, my woman may even fall behind. As to the franc, it seems to be holding steady. Still, with their record on the highways, no doubt a consequence of constricted lives, we can always expect a tragedy. At Easter, it was Pompidou's wife. I believe there was a prurient side to that event, photographs that were discovered, a sex ring. Though when I mentioned it to Madame, she flatly denied it.

How she loves it when the crime and scandal are chez moi! I remember the period of the assassinations. She was never happier. She understood the several deaths as a sign of developing instability. It was only a matter of time, she said, until our government would fall. She did not, of course, understand the checks and balances inherent in the system, nor our opposition to the Left. . . . Still, our news is an entertainment and distraction.

Madame Propre came with the apartment. At first, I was resistant to the idea. In my married life, I never had a maid. There were just the two of us and when the apartment was dirty, I cleaned it. I didn't realize the implications of what I was doing, not for myself, not for Benjamin. Only later did I remember my mother's words, "Anna, always have a maid, whether you need one or not." When I asked why, she replied, "On principle, Anna, on principle." I did not know what principle she meant. I only knew that as I was home, I could do the work myself. I had no temptation, even then, to go out, which is ultimately how I settled on my work. But my resistance seemed foolish. The woman's wages were insignificant, less than half of what it cost in America. Moreover, I had begun to see possible advantages. . . . My being home had created an expectation in Benjamin which interfered with my work. Little did I know then how I would be defending the very person I intended to serve his interest in my place!

Madame Propre had been with the family who owned our apartment for many years. As they were retiring to Provence, they were concerned about her. They wanted to talk to me. When the negotiations for the apartment were concluded, Madame Ambert asked if I would come again to discuss the matter. We sat on wooden benches in front of the fireplace. They were coffers, to be exact, from an old disbanded monastery, in Normandy, I think she said. (M. Ambert remained standing. He regretted he couldn't sit down. He would be leaving soon.) His wife spoke of their children, who were grown now. Madame Propre looked after them. Was I planning a family, she wanted to know.

Later, Madame Propre came by. By this time, the husband had gone, which was a relief. For, while he stayed, he had been hovering, shifting his weight from foot to foot, clearing his throat, as if to remind his wife she must get on with it, to which she would respond, "Oui, chéri, je le sais." The two women embraced. Would they have done so had he been there? I doubt it. No doubt, like many husbands, he resented an apparent closeness. When he was gone, Madame Ambert, mindful that it was I who was there to speak to her maid, found reason to excuse herself, disappearing into what is now Benjamin's bedroom to continue her packing. I could see that Madame Propre had been in tears. Her color was blotchy, purple veins showing through, her eyes revealed a definite strain. Her scrubwoman's hands turned nervously in her lap.

"Je veux rester," she began.

What could I say to her! "Oui, je le sais."

Silence followed. I attempted to explain: "Normalement, je fais le travail moi-même. C'est pour ça que j'hésite."

The truth is, I was reluctant to hire her. Could it have been that the relationship I witnessed did not leave room for me? Was I, like M. Ambert, the jealous one?

"N'hésitez pas," she then implored me.

A tear escaped, then another. I gave her my handkerchief. Then, between sobs, she let me know what it meant for her to continue to come and work here.

"Je ne suis pas contente chez moi."

I suggested there might be another family in need of her excellent services.

"Ce n est pas facile de trouver du travail." It is true that work is difficult to come by in Paris, particularly in a family which is reliable. And, in any case, how could I resist such genuine suffering? We came to terms. She would work four hours instead of the expected five, a compromise on her part, she said, for which I agreed to give her full pay on her vacations, more than making up for the loss in pay. . . . Sometimes, when I think about it, I wish she hadn't come. Without such services, my life would be different. But, I have grown used to her. Though I know now there are some people who shouldn't keep a femme de ménage. And that, perhaps, I am one of those people.

My mother had a maid once who didn't want to leave. Her name was Elsie. She lived on a poor side street in our neighborhood, which made our location a convenience. Like Madame, she could walk from where she lived. When we went out for dinner, she'd ask if she could stay. "You don't have to pay me," she'd say. My mother didn't like leaving her there. Elsie did not inspire confidence. Once, when we returned, my mother had forgotten the key so she had to ring the bell. Elsie didn't answer. . . . My mother didn't fear for her things. She feared for Elsie! So did I. I had been on an errand to where she lived, a rooming house, dirty and poor; the hallway, drab and unpainted; her room, one of a dozen on the floor. She lived with her son in a small room where they ate dinners cooked on a hot plate and got on each other's nerves, which was why she liked to work, I suppose.

Like many women who live in apartments in New York, my mother had left a key with a neighbor. On this occasion, the neighbor wasn't home. We went to the pay phone. Elsie didn't answer. In desperation, we contacted the super. Fortunately, he was there. With his master key, we went inside our apartment. What did we think to find? A corpse? No less. We looked everywhere. Could she have gone home? We called out.

In the end, we found her. She was in a back closet, washing the walls down with Spic and Span. True, the closet door was shut, which is why she couldn't hear us. But Elsie didn't need to explain. We understood.

Unlike my mother's Elsie, Madame Propre is professional. She knows that she does it for the money. Despite the tearful scene with Madame Ambert which implied attachment, loyalty, she does not let me forget the cost of little favors. For example, just today, she helped me with the shopping. Purchases were to be made in two different parts of town. When Madame came back, she had to say to me, "Ça pèse lourd." As if I didn't know the bag was heavy. Had I not carried it myself the week before? All the same, I acknowledged her complaint, said that I was grateful. But this was not enough! She continued to go on about it. She should have made two trips, she said, or, she would not have gone at all. I was sorry, of course. Very sorry. To make up for it, I insisted she take home with her an extra can of beans. "Prenez les deux," I said in the end, for I knew I could make the cucumbers instead.

To the matter of this dinner. . . . An old cousin and her husband, dottering remnants of prerevolutionary Russia, are our guests. I'll buy the caviar. I always do. We'll talk of their relations, of a country which no longer exists. We'll use words which are no longer current, the words my husband's parents used to use. Long ago, we had pressed chicken and string bean cakes in his parents' home. We were lovers then, in New York City, or should I say friends? Though on reflection, I think that neither term is accurate. For we came together joylessly, so as to get on with the business of our lives. Now his parents are dead, and in this city I am the stranger who, like them, remains outside the culture. There is nothing French about me, after all these years, though I do speak the language. Still, the ability to speak a language counts for little when it is my feelings that matter.

I used to resent seeing these cousins by marriage. It is not that they are almost in their graves that has changed my mind. I am not easily given to sentiment with family. It is that, increasingly, I feel more like them, of another world, on the way to Provence. When they are gone, and it won't be long now, there will be no more guests at our table.

I think of going back to America. But there is nothing there for me now. It's been so long. I do not speak the language easily. My English, like my America, is culled from the newspapers. And what about Madame! Who could I find there to shape my days, to force my mind away from the dreams fashioned from the classified section? She is strong and she is just. I leave my coffee cold in the cup and light more cigarettes than I smoke. I must be told that I am a waster. I waste coffee and cigarettes. I waste time. Madame Propre is herself a saver. She saves me money and time. She saves my days. For it is her nagging that drives me to the front pages of the paper, to my America, and finally to my work.

I translate novels; novels for the old ladies who never go out and for the young ones too. All my novels have happy endings. The secretary who has a shipboard romance paid for with her hard-earned wages is rewarded with a new image of herself. The widow with the job of raising three growing boys, finds happiness again. Promises, promises, the promise which in life is unkept is here invariably fulfilled. I offer these ladies the promised land in their native tongue and though I know better, I cannot help but believe in it too, at least for the hours in the morning when I happen to be turning it out.

This work was to be temporary, to carry us through leaner times, or so I told myself. I used to like to think what I did made a difference, despite my husband's disapproval: "Potboilers!" he said. "How will you be able to stand them?" He would have liked to keep me from these translations. But I pointed out that potboilers paid better. "Well," he answered begrudgingly, "I suppose it's all right for now." But I grew attached to the work and he to the money. And though I sometimes go through my desk drawers and look at old dreams, my poetry, my promise, I'm not really sorry. Why should I be? I am very good at my work, very quick. I work for a few hours only, which is enough. And if my gift for my own language is not what it once was, it doesn't matter. My language has become the language of cheap romance, and my dreams, the dreams of those unhappy ladies. I get my images from the can, I reject all but the prepackaged. And I have pride in my work, in its unfailing consistency. The more so, that it seems to translate itself. When I come upon a text, it is as if a well in me were opened up, bottomless in its depth. I cannot think it will run dry! Each day at my desk, the language pours out. It matters little my current mood or what has happened in the day. All that is not of the work dissipates. Time speeds up to a rapid pace. And when my pages are done, I am returned to my life with an energy I did not previously possess. The intransigence of early morning is gone and my mind is free. No. I would not stoop to pawn off my poetry on the readers now. My dreams take a more devious route. . . . Only last night, I dreamed that I was involved in a rescue operation. I am above an old abandoned quarry, slabs of granite lie about, tin cans everywhere, broken pieces of glass. It looks as if it has been used for target practice. I do not know where the quarry is located, or how I have come there. Out of the brush appears a group of boys such as might live on nearby farms, country boys gone plump from eating their mother's pies. They are looking at me. I want to get out of there. But there isn't anywhere to go. It does not seem they mean me any harm. What do they have in mind to do? Two of the boys, sandy-haired and freckle-faced, draw out cats from a burlap bag. Now they are making their way toward the lower quarry ledges near where there are diamond-shaped pools. "Wait!" I hear myself call out to them. "Please!" And I scramble down the ledges in their direction. "Give them to me!" They won't listen, but continue toward the water, flinging them like skipping stones in the dark pol-

11

luted waters. I do not wait but go in just as they are about to be submerged. The boys, broken with laughter, slapping their hands to their thighs, are above me on the ledges. Looking up, I see the insides of mouths, and I with my cats, trophies from some private war, step round them and go on.

It occurred to me to write it down but when the terror left, I thought better of it. Who, after all, would want to read it? Not my good ladies, who'd only be alarmed. I don't want to alarm anyone. I was relieved to return to my work.

Madame knows nothing of my work. She regards me as the fusty scholar type: an unserious woman, a waster of paper and typewriter ribbon. She doesn't concern herself further with that part of my life, nor would I have it otherwise. She would not talk to me as she does. She would have airs. I would be quelqu'une instead of plain madame. I could not bear that! "Combien ça coûte, ça?" she asks, when I've been to the store. For she drives me there with her special needs: the wood restorer, the spray cleaner for mirrors and windows, the chamois, the spot cleaner to remove the grease stains from the upholstery. I am ever mindful of the price, as if in some small measure I could pay her back for taking such trouble with me. I don't want to disappoint Madame. I wouldn't disappoint her for the world! If it were not for her intercession, would I struggle at all against the chaos which threatens my life? Would I go out?

As for my husband, he is rarely at home, save for occasional weekends. And when he is here, he doesn't

12

want to go out. He's been out. He's been all over the world, Tunisia, Morocco, the island of Curaçao. And when I speak to him, he often doesn't hear me. "What!" he answers, in his distraction. His mind is on other things. His work, I assume, which involves him in debits and credits, expenditures and profits. Time and money are the language of his concerns. . . . Sometimes I wonder, if he could reach across class interest and habits already established, would Benjamin and Madame Propre get on? Would they not share a common vision of the world, and yes, even of me!

I take another cup of coffee and look through the paper again. "Encore du café!" Madame is at me. "C'est pas bon pour l'estomac. Il vaut mieux boire du thé! C'est plus digestible. On peut mourir du café." Yes, I know how one can die of drinking coffee, Madame. The example of Balzac, scribbling his way out of debt, is ever before me. Only last week, I read findings from a recent cancer report. Coffee is on the list along with alcohol, cigarettes, two of your favorites, Madame. The list is longer than you know and may include some of your own favorites. The rind of the Camembert, the saucisson you love to eat.

Death and disasters! How she loves to imagine my death, the murder of the Canadian minister, the revolutionary shot at dawn in Brazil, sensing her own solidity in our violent ends. We form her pleasures which I cannot begrudge her. As pleasures of the mind, they do me no injury. If only she would lower her voice when she speaks! My nerves are ajangle. . . . But then, perhaps she is right about the coffee I drink and it is not her voice that does me in.

I go to my study and shut the door. There's pleasure in that.

I do on the average two novels a quarter. As I don't translate any longer for the money, there is no need to increase my pace, though sometimes I think that I'd like to, that, maybe, I should. Still . . . it's enough to fill those perilous hours from eleven to one, when Madame is here, hours in which, were I not so occupied, my mind would be plagued, if not by dreams or fantasies then by events or people. In the absence of my work, I'm made aware of the least little activity. A neighbor comes down the stairs. I think, right away, about which neighbor that might be. Is it M. Le Valois, for example? I can tell by the weight of the step. Or the widow who lives on the top floor? Her step is lighter and she pauses at the landing, which makes me wonder if Madame Valiant is getting enough to eat. She seems thinner. Is she shrinking? She is past sixty now. Or does she suffer from disease? For her sake, I'll be relieved when summer comes. . . . The widow has cats, five of them in all. Not that I see them. Although just last year, I did catch a white ball of fur on the stairs, which I carried back to her immediately. She asked me to stop in, which I did, though I didn't stay long. Under the eaves, in a straw basket such as is used for laundry in large families, I saw the rest of its family: a mother, four kittens in all, now that the vagrant was returned. . . . Does she not think to have the cat fixed? There are too many cats and not enough old ladies to feed them, or young ones either, for that matter. . . . I was, of course, concerned with what they ate. "De la viande," she assured me. "Vous payez cher?" I asked. Again, I was anxious. "Pas cher du tout!" I was relieved to learn scraps came from the butcher and that the expense was negligible. There must be dozens like her with whom our butcher deals. Are there scraps to go round?

I am glad to shut distractions out, to go into my study to work. I am a translator, I say, if only to myself. I have said it to Benjamin. How many times did I use work as my excuse? There was a period, but that was some years back, when the telephone rang. Women called, the wives of my husband's colleagues, asking me to join them for lunch; to work on a benefit performance for handicapped children; even to head a fund-raising drive for Korean orphans. This is what the American women must do abroad, or so they would tell me. "You will be known as much by the charity you serve as by the clothes on your back," said a Mrs. Kingman Brooder. Another, Mrs. Alice Van Leer, officious and round-bottomed, said, "We're a tightly knit group." Do your part was the message that she gave me. It was almost a threat. I had no intention of complying. I could have stayed in America to be in their league. Of course, I was an ideal target for such women, not having a child in the way. They felt obliged to lay claim on me for committee work and benefits. Here, more than in America, every passable American woman is asked to join. For some, that may be good, but not for me! They did not like letting me go my own way and said as much. Yet I withstood them and became anathema. To think I might have become some captured soul with no special qualities, making others' lives agreeable.

At first, Benjamin was ashamed of my refusal to meet such easy demands. He didn't understand where the demands would lead! But I had known women who did good works. My own mother headed the drives for muscular dystrophy, cystic fibrosis, cancer. I can't remember them all. When the drives were on, the house would fill with boxes and packets. Then her workers would arrive. "Darling" this and "darling" that, is what I heard. And the laughter! What was there to laugh about?

I stood firm and Benjamin came to accept the limits I set down. And then, I extended them. I would not travel with him, which was as well. Since, when I did go, I was forever a concern. Was I all right? Did I have something to do? What did I do? Why didn't I say where I'd been? . . . Such were my refusals that inevitably my husband began to be away more. And the women no longer called.

Benjamin said it would hurt his career but it hasn't. As he had his freedom, he could travel more than his colleagues. They saw advantage in that. He is little affected by my intransigence now. One could say that it is I who was responsible for his advancement. He is only a second vice-president but it is possible that he may become first vice-president! I would not deny him his hopes. It is still a long way from the bottom of the social ladder, an immigrant's son, a peddler's boy. To arrive at the happy point in his career even as second vice-president of one of our great American banks is a certain success. Is there a man of his acquaintance who does not envy him a little his freedom to come and go? He has my blessings. His is an enviable position. And if his wife does him no good as a hostess and a mother, she has added to the world's sense of his power. No one pities the man who does as he likes, least of all the man in question.

Though I don't earn a great deal (one doesn't here), I have saved money over the years. It is all in the bank under my maiden name. I do not choose to spend it. Rather, it has paid for my dreams.

It isn't as if I haven't had my own money. An allowance was settled upon me at the time of my marriage. And though the amount is meager in terms of the total estate left at my father's death, it is enough to guarantee a certain independence. Benjamin and I have divided our expenses. He paid for the apartment. My money took care of the improvements, the kitchen, the bathroom, furniture. But what comes out of my father's estate doesn't feel so much mine, not in the same way. Money that comes from my labor pleases me. Even that the labor be lacking dignity pleases me. That such work cannot be traded upon in the world is not a drawback. Quite the opposite. It becomes mine alone. The mechanical element, the stock of ready phrases stored in my brain, rather than boring me, is the source of my entertainment. When I come upon a new phrase, and that is rare in my work, I am delighted. I repeat it aloud and listen to it resonate. I give it other contexts. It can live in me for days. When I come up against the same phrase, again and again, uttered at the same moment by still another lonely soul about to be liberated from her pain, I am also delighted. I have unlearned my prejudices, the elegant economies of language to which I was born. How many can say of themselves the same? Not many, I am sure.

Sometimes I think of changing my life. Marriage does not agree with me. It is nothing personal. I do not like to couple. The way things have worked out, coupling is at a minimum. This is particularly necessary as to me coupling means giving up. I cannot say what it means for others. It is perhaps different. It must be or marriage would be abandoned. . . . I think of abandoning mine. But where would I go? I fear change even as I think of it. I have habits to which I am attached. I am attached to this room. I like looking out the window and watching the scene change. . . . Traffic is heavy at the beginning and end of the day. Trucks stopping and starting. The traffic jam and the horns begin their endless cacophony. In the afternoon, it is quiet until the evening, when the light changes. People come and go. I know most of the regulars, who, when I'm down there, sometimes nod at me. Occasionally, we pass the time of day. They notice I've been away. "Vous étiez en vacances?" they say. I answer yes or no, according to my mood, and we continue.

I notice that I am getting older. The hairpins, which never hurt before, sometimes give me headaches. I look at Madame and see that she is changing. Does she also look at me? America seems very far away. It would not be easy to go back. Who would I know? I did not like it before. . . . I lived on the East Side, near the river, on Ninety-second Street. Our apartment was number 1309, one of two on the floor. The other belonged to a Mrs. Ohman. Sometimes if no one was home, I waited for the return of my mother, who was out all the time, lunches, committee work. . . . Or I went down on the street. I remember being chased. Who does not remember being chased! He was a dirty old man. Perhaps he was harmless. Perhaps I never saw him at all. And I dreamed of summers in Maine when I would escape the phantoms of the street.

I leave Paris rarely. It is only in an idle moment, really, that I think of leaving at all. I go to the Midi in summer with Benjamin. The glamor and the bustle attract him. He thinks of when he was young. He watches bodies on the beach. There are plenty of bodies there. To go into the water, one must step over them. I dream of another spot by the sea with empty beaches and peopleless towns, perhaps in Brittany. He won't hear of going there. The water is cold. There is nothing to do.

I would think of summers in Maine if I were there. . . . Those in charge were not careful. I was out after dark. I might have drowned. I was alone. I got used to it, fond of it even. I am fond of it still. My father died. My mother had notions of trips abroad, of childless summers in exclusive resorts. I argued. She answered me: "You have nothing to say in the matter. You're too young to understand it's for your own good!" What did she know of my good? What did her lawyer know? Arguments were useless. The house was sold. The lawyer suggested summer camp as a kind of cure and there was no way out. I learned to play volleyball in the hot sun and move from activity to activity when the loudspeaker announced that it was time. I, who ran free, a wild uncared-for creature, as the lawyer described me, was put into uniform. I swam and rode, played tennis and volleyball. I wore brown and blue and learned to contain my rage, summer after summer after summer. I wasn't a great success as a camper and sometimes, when I wasn't asked back, my mother would get together with the lawyer to find another camp to take me in.

I have tried to go back to that empty beach ever since. In America, it's too late. There are no more empty beaches. Here, I am on a shuttle between Paris and the Midi. I dislike the heat of the south and the congestion. When I am there, I look at the beach from our villa but never go down. I go to Gassin to shop. It is quiet and empty of tourists. A few German families come back every summer. But they are inside walled gardens. Walking on the cobbled streets, I am aware of sandals flapping. There is usually a wind. I make what purchases I need, a piece of meat, some vegetables to put into a soup and I am on my way again.

The beaches in Maine are littered with paper now and houses cuddle up to the edges of the beach like five-and-dime-store necklaces and where the land is free of them, in state parks, there are campers, the endless rows of trailers and tents, the little stands which serve the needs of the campers and the inadequate blue accommodations containing the public shower and the toilet. I am saddened at the availability of those Maine beaches outside Ogunquit.

In the Midi it is the same. The campers come. Students from the lycées and the universities, tradesmen from London, schoolteachers from Devon and Hertfordshire, telephone company employees from Paris and Lyon. Once, Madame Propre came camping with her family. She brought their tent to the feet of Gassin, to my feet. I was in the hills above her as I always am, in the same rented villa we've had for years. She must have enjoyed looking up at the house she'd decided must be mine. To her family, she no doubt pointed out its distinguishing features, a large terrace, shade trees, a little iron bench. I never saw her. But she let me know in Paris she'd been there. That now she knew that landscape as well as I do. Better, perhaps. For she went around from place to place with her children, climbing castle ruins, visiting churches, picking up mementos of the trip, an ashtray marked Saint-Tropez, a packet of photographs, some yardage of material to have made into a dress. I am sure Madame cleaned up their campsite, even going so far as to glare at the adjacent campers, moving them to do the same, lesser mortals from the north, perhaps, who relaxed and expanded in the hot Mediterranean sun, leaving papers and wine bottles in their wake. Madame, cleaning up as she went, made order of her life then on that holiday as she makes order of mine now, cleaning up messes, signs of indulgence and fruitless time.

There is nothing out of place when she is here. But when she is gone, papers lie on the floor where they fall. Clothes accumulate on the two side chairs. I do not bother to hang them up. I wait for Madame. When she comes my garbage pail will be cleaned out, my wastebaskets emptied, my toilet cleaned. I will watch her take the signs of my indulgence away, the overflowing ashtrays and the half-emptied coffee cups crusted over with mold, so that I may begin again when she is gone. Occasionally, lines of censure form round her mouth, and I hear her mutter under her breath, "Quelle cochonnerie!" I make an effort for a day or two and relapse again. . . . Oh, Madame. I wonder if you need my chaotic nature to impose your own meticulous and painstaking order upon! What if there were no mess? Would your life tumble around you as mine does around me in your absence?

I am tired now. I'd like to think that I might find some other beach where there is no litter, where there will be no athletes reaching for the ball across a net, no children on summer holidays led on to the beach by parents burdened with the latest snorkling equipment, balls, plastic boats and seating arrangements, identifying themselves with the season's newest polka-dot umbrella. This is not the beach I want. My beach will be empty, and the only sound will be that of the waves breaking against the shore and the birds squawking for their dinner.

Madame is putting away her tablier and slippers. Au revoir, Madame. "Au revoir, Madame. A demain!" She joins the crowd below my window. I watch her disappear. My husband will be home tonight. He's made a special effort to be here. He called me long-distance and I was very compliant. I wonder how much longer it will take him to discover that my compliance is perhaps only another form of sabotage. Maybe he knows it already and doesn't care. Or maybe it is I who am past caring and cannot be bothered to probe my feelings. Sometimes I like to think that refusal is the mystery that sustains me. Anyway, his cousins may not come again. They are very old now. I feel a strange pleasure in the thought that this last link of the flesh will be broken too.

2

Cousins

Benjamin is in his room. His door is shut. I am in mine. Our kiss was mere formality.

"How was Spain?" I asked.

"Hot, muggy." He takes off his jacket and tie and sits down, weary, expressionless.

"Did your business take long?"

"Not very long. You see that I'm here."

There have been too many returns to speak about. We are neither one of us eager to talk.

"And what about you?" He doesn't forget to ask, to seem to care.

"I finished the manuscript."

"Already!"

This is of interest, a sign of activity. I think he imagines I do nothing in his absence, that this work I speak about is only a fiction. Because he has not himself fingered the pages, their reality is in question. I have noted the absence of response to the work itself. He hasn't asked which book was completed or what it's about! This is really too bad as I should have liked to talk to him. The subject is marriage. The wife, who represents the author, I assume, is the victim of neglect. She has kept a life going despite her husband, for the children's sake. In the end, he dies of a terrible disease, the wife beneficiary of a large insurance policy. It is a pretty fiction, moving to the point of tears.

"Did you go out today?"

Never content with what I say, he is scrutinizing.

"Of course I went out. I bought dinner. I got cleaning supplies. Madame gave me a list!"

"Madame and her lists! I'd like to tell her what to do with her lists. Ever since she came here, her needs have intruded on my life."

This bodes ill for our evening. I will attempt to placate him.

"It is her price! Think of all she does for us!"

He does understand that we need her, and so will contain this misdirected petulance.

Madame Propre also has a temper. She bristles, on occasion threatens to leave.

"Je n'aime pas mon boulot. Je vais prendre ma retraite sans plus attendre."

I am also the one to appease her.

"Je vais vous donner le double d'argent pour les vacances!" To double or triple her vacation pay is easy enough for me to do. What does it come to? An extra fifty dollars.

Sure enough, her anger subsides. She is imagining a new machine, a winter coat for herself and daughter. . . . They are walking arm in arm down the rue de Rivoli on a Sunday afternoon. All are in awe of their well-clad figures. They are, of course, wearing new clothes, having stretched the budget to include shoes and pocketbooks, new skirts as well, all of the finest quality!

"Are they sisters?" she hears a particular gentleman say, not your common shopkeeper, a lawyer, perhaps, on his way to lunch having been in session all week over at the Palais de Justice. You can tell by his shoes, expensive, shining. She calls her daughter's attention to them. . . . Brought to the end of a reverie, Madame Propre remembers her situation. She has been insulted by the husband of her employer. I must do more than offer money. An apology is what is wanted. Very well then, I'll oblige her.

"Mon mari, il travaille trop." She should understand that! "Il est de mauvaise humeur!" This receives a slight acknowledgment from Madame. "Il est désolé de vous rendre malheureuse!" Now she's listening. Her look is softening. She has always longed for his respect. Hence, my words are doing their work and she is restored to me.

"Je reste pour vous, mais pas pour le monsieur!" She explodes her words on target like little gems.

Madame Propre now picks up her torchon; with a

kind of care that is appropriating, she whisks away what particles of dust remain on the mantel. The incident is over.

I do not want difficulty. I want . . . I will not think what I want now. Cousins are coming, bringing with them petits fours and a magnum of champagne. It is very dear now. On the telephone, I had asked them not to bring it.

"Non," answered the husband, "jamais le champagne!"

It was a mistake. But I am aware of how little they possess, a mere pittance to live on, and in Paris, squeezed into rooms hardly above ground level. . . . Sergei deserves better! Peddling to restaurants the delicacies he must himself forgo. And Luba, the little woman who waits for him, looking to please, not knowing how. Did she say something wrong? Should she smile now? Yes now?

But I resist them no more. I want the evening to go well. I'll compliment the champagne and be effusive over the petits fours. We'll talk of the summer. Will they be going to the Auvergne? They will. And again to the same hotel? Of course, for they are known to the proprietors and treated well. After all, they help to fill the inn, which is good business, the more so when times are slow. But will they come back from the Auvergne? The question is neither to be asked nor answered this night.

The table is set. I've taken out the candelabra left to me by a favorite relation, my father's mother's sister, a rather pretty woman, petted and loved. . . . Once, when

I was admiring them on the sideboard in her dining room, she said: "Marry and you shall have them."

One of the many instructions to that end.

Tonight, the candelabra will remind cousins of better days, in Georgia, the happiness to which they would awake. Luba, listening to her husband, head bobbing, eyes shining, will confirm the dream. Sergei, moved by the sight of a wife who has shared his life, will offer the toast. We'll drink to Luba, the little sister of his war-hero friend. Long-dead brother whose photographs and medals remain on their tables and walls, speaking of a glory to which they are attached. . . . I remember going to the apartment. It was when we first came to Paris. That day, it was raining. Sergei was outside to meet us. As the taxi approached, he moved to open the car door, offering his umbrella for our protection. Quickly, he whisked us into the passageway by which we approached their apartment. All the while, he was telling us of his desire for a better apartment, a second-floor apartment which would let in a view. And they should like a bit of sun. But they are still looking, he said. I thought at the time that perhaps he was ashamed of where they lived, ashamed before us. In particular, he wanted us to know that where they were living didn't truly represent them. The apartment consisted of two painfully small rooms, an alcove for a kitchen. It was neat. Like Luba herself, who couldn't do enough, offering us hors d'oeuvres, cheese, luscious sorts of fruit, tidying up as she went.

But I hear footsteps. The elevator is out of use again.

They want the tenants to buy a new one. M. Le Valois is in charge of the matter. And it is right that he should be! The building was formerly his grandmother's, a lady who lived grandly, he said, in the manner of the last century. But the tenants haven't come to an agreement. My neighbor down below me feels that the old elevator should be repaired again. When M. Le Valois pointed out that it would continue to break down, he shrugged his shoulders and said, "What of that!" Such an attitude is not surprising as he lives on the second floor. As for myself, I don't mind, either way. I'd as soon walk. To tell the truth, I'm a little afraid of the elevator. But it is hard on the aged Luba. They stop at each landing. She leans heavily on Sergei who is used to her weight. Her health has never been good. Her circulation is poor and she must wear a special stocking on her right leg to support a varicosity. They continue. . . . They pause again on the landing below me. . . . And they are here.

"Bonjour, Luba. Sergei. Ça va bien, j'espère."

"Ça va, ça va."

Sergei the kisser, wets my cheeks. Not Luba, dry-mouthed from strain. It cost her to come out tonight. Were it not for Sergei, she would have said no. Is it her arthritis again? The pinched nerve? And what about the varicosity? Will they or will they not have to operate?

As usual they are talking a mélange of French and their native tongue. No need to give way entirely, letting the perfectly good words, not worn out to them, sink to the bottom.

Benjamin is behind me. He doesn't fail them in his

greeting. Cousins in Paris can be dear. Arms out, he no doubt thinks of his parents. And when they are gone, he'll puff at his cigar until even I am asleep in my bed. His arm is on my shoulder, wanting to reassure them. Sergei, looking into my eyes, sees a little. Now he presses my hands.

"Ça va, ma petite, vous pouvez confier à moi."

In me, he sees a companion in suffering.

"Ça va, Sergei, ça va."

He would speak to me of deeper matters, the misery behind a smile, but can't. This is as far as we will go. A peddler of dreams gotten from jars of caviar can't really speak of what is knotting the heart. I forgive you, Sergei. I would forgive myself but am caught in a posture as are we all. Never mind. I am determined to please, to be pleasing.

"Vous êtes toujours jeune, Sergei!"

It is true that he looks young compared to Luba. It is partly his energy. His desire to enter in. And it is also his compact figure, his full head of hair, unusual in a man of his years.

"Ce n'est pas vrai, chérie. Vous me flattez!"

He may say that I flatter him. Well, so I do! Is there another gift that I can offer?

We've always observed the vouvoiement, though lately, as they are on the way to Provence, I've wanted to tu-toyer. Yes. There is the formal *you* in Russian, but it allows greater intimacy. Yet the sudden change would shock and so the vouvoiement must do though it does not sit well with me vis-à-vis cousins. But why make so much of the forms? Can they matter? Still, I feel the disjuncture, call it a rift, between feeling and expression, making me think it might be better not to speak.

Luba sits, hands folded in her lap. At seventy, still the good girl, lest one doubt; back straight, glance downward, no trouble, never was. Nuns' work, I think. Absolution, the rock pile in the corner or rapped knuckles, perhaps. One has heard stories. And I know for a fact she was in a convent. . . . Once, her sweetness, cloying to me, made it so I disliked her touch, the faint smell of camphorated garments little aired coming up at me. Despite a liking for Sergei, I was unable to modify the aversion. . . . I advance. Now I see how Sergei transforms this drab sister into an emblem of a hero-brother, barren and disappointing though she may have been to him, allowing me to overcome a distaste. Children, cleansed by an attitude, do as much. . . . I remember a child. It was by the chestnut vendor parked outside school at the first sign of winter. This child denied the blackness of another in the group.

"Why she's as white as you or I!"

I knew better, answering her back: "She isn't. She's black as coal!"

I have long since given up being forthright.

I pass the hors d'oeuvres and observe that Benjamin is studying me. He perhaps wonders why I am so gracious to them. Why them and not himself, he would like to know. Does it have meaning for him? They are his family. Can it point to a change in our relations? A change for the better, perhaps?

"In Georgia, the land was rich."

It is Sergei, in an expansive mood. I will take my seat by the fire where it is warm.

"I studied in the gymnasium."

If he has had an education, why hasn't he done better? The question, how it is that some do well in their adopted country and others not, has long puzzled me. There is a theory which may apply in such a case. Leaving, in certain cases, may be too great a shock to recover from.

"Life was good for me and my family."

Perhaps, Sergei, it only seems good in the remembering! It is that way for me, I know. Here, on the other side of the ocean, it is easier to feel expansive, to allow a rosy glow to settle over parts of my life.

"Then came the revolution!"

Poor Sergei! He might have been an ornament in such a scheme. I can see him presiding over meetings of his fellow workers. Honorary chairman of the program committee! Master of ceremonies. And how they would have loved him! Rewarded at the various stages of his career, he would have taken pride in what he'd done. And such pride would have been justified. What a misery to be denied his proper destiny by a quirk! Transporting love of country here . . . I see in his manner how he suggests a grandeur to do with there! And Luba. How happy she would have been, turning collars round, darning socks, sewing the seams fast, lest they not be ready on time.

Now we are to hear about the escape. It is one of his finer stories in which the obstacles encountered point to the prowess of the teller.

"Il y avait des montagnes, des rivières, des villages, c'était long. Il y avait des moments quand j'ai pensé, c'est la mort qui me gagnait." His handkerchief is out. We are to admire his capacity for feeling. Are we not impressed by what the human being is capable of when endangered? Bravo, Sergei! Our glasses are raised for the toast.

"Nous sommes la continuation de la vie comme il faut!"

I suppose he is an old fool and that I delude myself about his qualities, or is it because these dinners are nearly done that I allow myself to dote on them? Yet, I cannot help but admire the man. What if his story is a pack of lies? (This has been suggested.) What he wants is to be part of a drama and so do I. His lies are his embellishments, they enhance the parties they represent.

Benjamin and I don't lie. We coexist. He in his world and I in mine. We observe the forms. He concerns himself with my health; it has not always been good. My stomach, my head, the way the phlegm can sink down into my chest, an old weakness. He has shown me kindness. I have done what I could. His meals are prepared. His papers are as he leaves them. I keep out of his way when he is working. On his return, clothes are made ready for wearing. And when he needs me, I am at his disposal, within limits. . . . Tonight, we pretend to do more, seeing in the aged pair, parents. Now that parents are dead, that a marriage may be ending (there has been no acknowledgment but it is so), I can allow myself such a dinner. Could I have done this for his parents? I have thought about the matter. Had I tried, they could not have accepted the gesture. Our table would have become a battleground for their son. And in the end, they would have possessed him with their Russian and their carriers of food. Tonight, I perform a role I was denied, playing, for just a little while, the good wife, the good daughter, reaping what profits I can.

I see Benjamin warms to me a little with the meal. I smile. But not for a minute do I think of building on that warmth. There was a time, but that was long ago, when I would have waited for a response from Benjamin, from parents, from the stranger in the street. Even so. In New York, while walking on Fifth Avenue or along the East River in my old neighborhood, I'd search out the sympathetic stranger and meet his eye. Most often, eyes averted mine or failed to see the challenge. Occasionally, not more than three times, there was a response. Only then did I experience the shock of my demand and run. Yes. I was a would-be heroine myself, needy, episode-making. That chapter, admittedly overlong, has come to an end. And yet, even as I plot the change, I am at it again! I've spilled the champagne! The meal is a shambles. Benjamin is getting out of his chair. He cannot abide such clumsiness. Very well then. I think I do it for him! But am I sure? Might it not be that the dinner is a mistake, the accident, my way of undoing it? Is this not some unwitting savage effort to undermine the cousinship? This is possible. I have made much of them, against all sense. What are they to me, if I deny this marriage? Two old people on the way to Provence, pretending to a relationship. And for what? Some half-baked idea of continuity? But now I must play out the scene.

Sergei, first to respond in all circumstances, reaches for my hand. "Ce n'est pas rien ma chérie. Moi, j'adore le champagne avec le poulet. Pas toi, Luba?"

Luba, mouth agape before the catastrophe, cannot answer. It is too much for her. Sergei must go on alone.

"C'est peut-être même agréable avec la salade. Mais peut-être vous préféreriez des petites assiettes?"

Not waiting for an answer, Sergei, with his grandest flourish, whisks away the dinner plates. Silence descends over the table. From the kitchen, there is the sound of cupboards opening and closing. It is Sergei looking everywhere for the salad plates. I will not move to help him. Indeed, I cannot. Meanwhile, Luba, with bowed head, seems to be drifting off, into reverie, perhaps? No. She gives out a profound snore.

The errant husband returns with sponge and mop. Perhaps he thinks to confuse us with the practical. His activity—he is now mopping up—disturbs the sleeper. She is shaken out of a dream. Now Sergei is returning with the plates. Luba looks on approvingly. Her good nature seems misplaced. She is clearly out of it now.

"Luba, Luba," says Sergei, demanding that she pay attention to him. She sits up, attempting to help him with the table. Sergei, while helping Benjamin, turns his attention to me with now an arm-patting, now a hand-squeezing. Benjamin, his mouth forming silent epithets, shows me his frustration at the distance between us. If I were nearer, I would feel it in the shins, a bruise that would stay with me for days.

With the mess taken care of, we can now resume the meal, I suppose. Not yet. Benjamin, looking on at his relations, is about to offer a toast. He is clearing his throat.

"Il y a encore du champagne."

This is more than I would have expected. Perhaps he is of their world, after all!

"A la vôtre!"

There is a general lifting of glasses, save for mine.

Sergei will counter with a second toast.

"A la prochaine fois!"

A la prochaine fois! I say there'll be no next time! Can't he see that!

Sergei repeats the toast in Russian, hoping to distract from my rebellion. His words, meant to give me time, I'm sure, have created a silence to which I must respond. And so I will.

"A la prochaine fois!"

Now, for the inevitable apology.

"Il faut m'excuser ce soir, Sergei, Luba. J'ai mal à la tête. Je suis désolée."

Thank God for indispositions, though any excuse would have done. It is the words that are wanted, concessive, easing.

"Ce n'est pas rien, chérie. Mais ta pauvre tête! Peut-être tu serais mieux au lit."

My God, he tutoie's me! The dear man! And yet, I, with my complication, cannot.

"Je reste avec vous."

The conversation turns to illness. I ask after Luba's health. She is delighted to tell me that she suffers. The mornings are terrible. It is her back, in particular, that forces her to take rests. Does she favor the use of heat, I want to know. I have had good luck with it myself. She has tried it, of course. But nothing besides rest can help. . . .We move on now and talk of Sergei's dwindling accounts. Yes, he is still handling certain products for the Russian restaurants, though he will be closing out now in all but two. Both the Montparnasse restaurant and the one across from the mosque in the seventeenth desire that he continue until he goes. They know him so well. He is like a friend. Only the other day, he was invited in for tea. The headwaiter, a fellow he's known for many years, asked after Luba.

Luba smiles and looks down at her hands. Now they exchange glances. They are ready to go. Luba, leaning heavily on Sergei, turns in my direction.

"Sergei, il a raison. Vous seriez mieux au lit!"

How kind she is to me! I don't believe we have ever understood each other before! I can go on now. I will ask them to stay.

"Je me sens mieux. Je veux que vous restiez. On peut finir le dîner, quand même." I put my arms around the two of them, and usher them back to their seats.

Benjamin, who has been out of the room for some time now, returns with my pills. There is no pill for what ails me! But we can settle our business later.

I fetch the salad from the kitchen. Now to ask Sergei about his escape from Georgia. He should not leave before the story is done. I know how the nostalgia will feed him. Better than wine, it will restore the light. I do not like it when the light is gone from his eyes because of me. It has been a difficult hour. Will we ever get beyond it? At last, he has begun his account. Already, they are over the mountains and into France. Now he is at the part where Benjamin's father comes in. It is the most difficult part to tell. For it is now we learn that he was to continue with him to America. That he did not is a sore point. How will he get round it?

"A Paris j'ai trouvé Luba, la petite soeur de mon cher ami. Ce n'etait pas possible d'aller plus loin. Votre père m'a compris, je vous assure."

He takes Benjamin's hand. Is he not here in his father's stead? For Sergei, he is. And the guilt that is Sergei's must be assuaged. Not to have gone on to America, to have remained in a country that never could feed him. As if America could have done better! But that he doesn't know, of course, which is too bad, as the illusion is a painful one. Come to think of it, had he not imagined his little tragedy in terms of not going on to America, he would have had to take on the burden of failure himself.

His eyes are filled with tears now, the bitter and the sweet. For while he has not made his way professionally, he has at his side an adoring wife. Luba, sister of his dead friend, emblem of a glorious moment, not his, of course, but a friend's.

Sergei grips Benjamin's hands more tightly than before. It is all he can do to control himself from absolute breakdown. His wife is crying too now. For is it not the story of their life, she, his silent partner, joined to him until death?

Poor Benjamin! His is not a part he can fulfill. Sergei's emotions are too large for him, too grandiose. Georgia is not my husband's country or his way. There has been a thinning of the blood in the generation that separates them, not to mention an apparent cultural difference America produces. For Sergei, happily, it is enough that his cousin be close. He does not see his discomforts, that Benjamin wants the story to end! But Sergei draws toward a conclusion now.

"Je me suis senti bien dans ma peau côté d'elle."

Luba looks down at her hands, trembling now with the palsy of old age.

Never mind that it is a pack of lies. Does it matter if Luba is younger or older than Sergei, if Benjamin's father was able to understand why his cousin stopped short of coming with him to America? Hasn't Sergei reaped a hundred times his reward for little lies, call it the necessary fiction, the fiction which is binding.

I intend to devote myself to such fiction, call it lies if you will, lies like Sergei's that take away from the pain of existence. In particular, I think of the pain of the would-be heroine who has fallen upon a script that is wanting. Alternatives are not always easy save between the covers of a book. Here is my part. Translations aid in the creation of flights, comings together, happy or violent endings. In reading, we can approach the desired action, learn it a little and retreat into the comparative safety of the known. When I think of my readers in need, many of them women like myself, I am moved to increase the number I take on. I might do four novels a quarter, even five, translations becoming my good works. I might give up doing tracts altogether, until now a sideline of mine. For I know that tracts fire the mind, releasing anger, even causing war. Think of the various manifestos. I put into a separate category those that have to do with art, which are harmless enough, restricted in their effect to a mere few thousand. While my novels sell in the millions! Wherever I go, in the railway stations and the airports, in every little drugstore that there is, they are there, on display in paperback.

But the meal is over. I have done all I can. Have I not banished the memory of wandering attention? Rebellion? Now I must have time to myself. They see that I am tired. But how to arrange it! I know. I'll clear the table. That failing, I'll rattle the dishes in the sink. There must be a way! But one last cigarette to give me courage. ... And now to begin. Plates first. Platters second. Now the silver and the glasses. Sergei, seeing my purpose, carries in what is left, trying all the while to catch my glance. He wants to be with me. I might have known it all along. Stop it, Sergei. You go too far. Leave me alone!

I have only so much energy for the world. Though I do not want to be mean, I have no choice. This last piece of business has made me angry. I had to push him away. I suppose he meant to console me, or maybe, to console himself. What does it matter now? I only know I want them to go. I must rest. I long for it! The sheer effort I've expended, the shopping, the cooking, the conversation too, have taken a toll, to be sure; going through an evening like this with Benjamin is less than ideal. Perhaps they will forgive me in the end.

Now on to the thank-yous and good-byes.

"Ah Sergei, Luba, vous voyez comme il est. C'est la nervosité, j'en suis sûre. Je me fatigue."

"C'est vrai, ce que tu dis, chérie. J'espère que ça ira mieux demain."

We kiss. The irrepressible Sergei would press himself against me. Even Luba is especially warm in her good-bye.

"A bientôt," I say.

And the inevitability is set into motion.

They are on the landing now, with Benjamin. I can hear them talking, though it would be as well if I could not. It is my husband who speaks.

"On a assez d'argent, mais elle veut travailler. C'est inutile d'en discuter davantage."

He complains of my working. All failings are ascribed to it. . . . It is good they believe in its demands! I too believe in them when I can. Sometimes it is difficult to believe in the work. A text reads poorly, or it only makes provisional sense. Worse, I doubt the value of what I am doing. But when I can, and I am able, I devote to my translations my very best efforts. I become involved in questions of style, choice of words and phrases, wonderful hack phrases for hack emotions. I say there is a need for such work and I attach an importance to it beyond mere relationship this never doubt. I separate out only my maid. Only she is truly necessary to my life. For she is my defense against the encroachment of filth, coffee crusting with mold, ashtrays spilling over, laundry which would otherwise lie stinking where it fell, and that she does it, ordering my life as my house, is my delight. . . . But wait! There is laughter outside the door. Benjamin has covered for me. The rushed departure, all is to be righted by this last analysis of me, cousin by marriage, after all.

The walk down is always easier. They continue without pausing. I hear the buzzer sound. Now the heavy door swings open and they are all out on the street.

Now I can smoke my cigarette in peace!

3

Other Relations

Cousins! What are these? They who know how to mark the coincidence of interests, the state's, theirs. I am mulling over their remarks which concern their reasons for moving somewhat earlier than they had planned. The redevelopment of certain areas of the city has been going on for some time now. (There are those who say I would not recognize New York. Paris, too, has changed.) For some who observe it here, it is an entertainment. In my neighborhood, particularly, people come to watch the dismantling and contemplate the wreckage. I have seen them stand silent before what they see. I have heard giddy paroxysms of laughter. Some do not care at all. It does not touch their lives. They have no connection with those who must go not to other parts of Paris, but beyond. These are the privileged citizens of this or any city. Where the cousins live is scheduled to disappear as a residential area. It is consigned to industry. My own section is designated for business, which is better by virtue of being cleaner, but those who will be displaced do not think so. We here do not know the details yet. Though I know it will not affect me, if I stay. It cannot as I live in what has been termed an historical monument, an expression which is loose in its meaning, I suppose, so as to give room to the ones who make their influence felt. I wonder who has influence here? This building remains a living space, one of the few that will stand. I know where Madame Propre lives, they think to make offices for government workers. That is in the Marais, where so much will be changing. Here, only the ones who die off or are squeezed out through lack of funds will be going. I think of my neighbor with the cats who, like the cousins, will be priced out. I think of what the cousins said tonight: "Mieux changer, mieux aller en Provence."

I know what will happen if they do not. They will be taken, dead or alive, they'll be taken and put in an area earmarked for the no longer employable. The ball and chain have already begun to swing in the quarter where they live and the factory whistle reminds those who do not work that they cannot stay. I have been through there, recently. I happened to be coming by taxi from another part of town. I asked the driver to stop and let me look. (I don't drive anymore. But I did. I had accidents, a fender, a back end, never a head-on collision. Taxis will do now to get where I need to go to see, to bear witness.) The workers punch in, punch out, or it's off to remote buildings, high rises, "gratte-ciels," is what they call them here. Unless they move on to Provence like the cousins. Of course, it is better to leave now than be shoveled up into newly constructed areas of asphalt and concrete, sparse, not what they are used to, not any of them who live lives rooted in neighborhoods with shade trees, parks where they sit on benches watching the young come and play. But I should look on the situation of the cousins positively. They do. They will enjoy a milder climate in a village. They did say they will be living in a village. . . . Someone goes, someone comes. The young come to cities in search of jobs, the old must leave for the lack of them.

But why should I think of cousins who are but mocking configurations of characteristics vaguely parental? I am no daughter more nor hardly wife, merely essence of such, which these cousins bring out. This will be over when I am gone from here, which I will be, soon.

Benjamin is down there now with the cousins, as if it matters that he is. It doesn't. For it cannot make him more what he seems and isn't. We can neither of us fill the roles of daughter and son here, much less husband and wife. People leave their country for reasons. Nostalgia confuses when oceans separate, and one thinks one can slip back. . . . I did tonight and I am tired for it. So now I will go to my bed. But if Benjamin insists, if I must, I'll take out my words, polished, tight, and hurl them, heavier than bricks, sharper than swords, meaner than devils, at him.

Bad morning in Paris, grisly and gray. Madame Propre comes grumbling into my room with the coffee, her tablier the same as yesterday, also her eternal scuffs which she must have left out yesterday to annoy me. I had to put them away, which was a provocation as they stink! Madame, you see you yourself are not free of the human corruptions! How I should like to speak to you about it. But I won't, for I know too well where it will lead!

"Votre café."

"Merci, Madame."

She will not speak to me but is shuffling off. The cousins coming has disturbed her routine. Rooms which are otherwise clean or familiarly dirty, are now ravaged. I hear her rattling round in there, the scene of a skirmish, I will not say battle. Dishes in the sink and food on the counters. Who could eat all? And I hadn't the will to do more. Under the table are the crumbs and the bits. The champagne was cleaned up. But there are bottles on the buffet, wine now turning to vinegar, uncorked and undrunk, nor will it be unless I have a go at it, which I won't, knowing too well how wine attacks the stomach and the head.

I am sitting on a large and comfortable Louis Quinze, not that it matters, save that my arms follow the arms of the chair, curving downward to hands which are idle now, though they won't be soon, not when I reach for a pen from the pen box, black, painted, pretty. This, I purchased on one of my walks. I do take walks and buy things, having the use in mind or the pleasure, as now, sliding the box out from its cover which is lacquered, black. The surface is cracked now. Never mind. . . .But my being used to this pen box and chair or the angle at which my back is when my head looks down toward the page is a matter of consequence, now that I think of leaving here.

Benjamin mounted the stairs four or five at a time. I felt he was mounting me, demanding, sexual.

"Bitch! How could you!"

"How could I what?"

"You know very well what! How dare you pretend to be innocent!" He is speaking to me from the other side of the door, which is locked. Thank God I thought to get a key!

"Now you've done it!"

"Done what? I thought I heard you all laughing!" I was referring to what took place at the foot of the stairs, a smoothing over when the cousins were leaving. I assumed if there was laughter, everything was all right.

"Some laughter! It cost me blood. They'll never come again. And I don't blame them!"

"You needn't have invited them."

"But this is my house. And you're my wife! Some wife! I don't know why I ever married you!"

There is much he means and doesn't say. For example, he is dissatisfied with this arrangement. Is he satisfied in another? If so, he should content himself. If not, he should look to himself for the cause. His opportunities are manifold but it is hardly my place to tell him so! Rex tyranneous!

When I was a child, I had a room at the end of a long hallway. And when a parent called out to me in anger, I pretended not to hear. So if the wish to confront was strong in them, they'd have to come to me. Although the approach was long, the apartment a duplex, the distance was no protection. I dreamed of a room of my own where no one could find me, where the separation from the real world was greater than any mere hallway could provide or stairs or floors. Somehow, I never found such a room. For, in the intervening years, there were roommates and lovers and finally what was once a wish became a fear and I was married.

If one was a certain age at a certain time, one married. Some months, a year even, might precede the event, but not more. I do not recall in what circumstances we acknowledged the inevitability. (Perhaps this will be taken as an evasion and I should therefore include a scene in which a decision so important to the unfolding of this story takes place. I say "decision" rather than "proposal" because the word more accurately reflects the manner in which we moved along from point to point. Actually, we were sitting on a bench, waiting for the train when the subject came up. Little was made of it, as we shall see. I think I said:

"Do you suppose we'll ever marry?"

It was an idle moment as I had nothing in mind. Benjamin thought a minute and answered back: "I guess so."

Just then, our train came and we continued on our way.)

I think of another train ride. We were going to meet my prospective parents-in-law. Then, I was aware of shapes and smells, of the fat-legged woman opposite, of the smudgy-faced child on her lap, and there were strap-hangers, strong-smelling, and Benjamin beside me. He was very quiet. His book was open but his eyes were unseeing. Every now and again he'd look up at the signs above the windows on the opposite side but I knew he was thinking and that his thoughts were a trouble to him. I wanted to engage him so that I might know more of what it was I would meet. For I knew virtually nothing up to this point.

"Is it about them?" I asked, for this much was obvious.

He nodded.

"Are you afraid they won't like me?"

This fear had entered my mind, as it was many months after our decision to marry that the meeting was arranged.

"No, it's not so much that as the ordeal itself. They'll have trouble with you, all right. They'd have trouble with anyone. It's just I wish I knew I was going to feel above it."

"Above it?" I repeated, hoping that he would say more.

"Yes. They can really get under my skin. You'll see."

We rode in silence for a while. But when we came out of the tunnel and I could be heard above the noise of the train, I tried to continue the conversation.

"Perhaps I shouldn't have come."

"You had to come. It's part of the deal."

"Maybe we could have met somewhere, in a restaurant. My mother would have been happy to arrange it." That it would have pleased my mother, I knew.

"They wouldn't have come. What they want is to have us there. In that way, they hold an advantage."

I was impressed with this understanding and wanted it for myself that I might be better prepared for this encounter. But though I understood the words, they did not help me any. He would not say more, though I asked, as if, in the speaking of what so closely concerned him, and now me, he might give away something much better earned.

They were, by comparison with other parents I had known, older, grayer, poorer. But this gave them an advantage in my eyes, for I was disposed toward difference in such a case. Finding something positive to attach myself to, I felt considerable relief and looked to make the best of the long afternoon ahead.

My introduction took place in the corridor, no more than a person wide.

"This is Anna," Benjamin said.

"Well," answered the father, "you're a fine-looking girl. But can you cook?"

We all laughed, even the mother, who otherwise seemed quite serious.

I took a quick look around. To the front of me, I saw a small, gray, rectangular living room, to the left, a kitchen, lighter, white, shining like a hospital laboratory. Indeed, its condition looked no less sanitary. Down the end of another narrow hallway, going toward the rear of the apartment, was the master bedroom. It struck me as odd that there was no second bedroom, for it was in this place, I understood, that my future husband had grown up. It took a while to understand that the gray living room had been his room as well and that the green couch I was by then sitting on was more than likely his bed. And yet I knew that his people were not poor, that his father did well enough, in the way of things. How then explain accommodations in which there was no place for a child?

We sat in the living room, Benjamin and I on the couch, his father on a kitchen chair opposite.

"So tell me about your family," his father began. "Where was your mother from. And your father?"

"My mother was born in New York," I answered. "My father is from Saint Louis, originally. His family moved here when he was a child."

"And what about your grandparents?" he asked. "Where did they come from?"

"They were also born here."

"Well, where did their parents come from?" he continued.

"From Vienna, I think."

"Vienna? Don't you mean Poland?" he asked.

"I don't think so. I'm not sure."

I could tell he was dissatisfied with my answers. But the truth was, I knew very little about my family. We did not speak about family at home. Perhaps what came before was not an issue. Or were they interested in erasing the past? If so, why? I didn't know the answer. In any case, they had kept their stories from me.

Meanwhile, Benjamin's mother, aproned and occupied, would come in and out with an ashtray or an offering, whisking away the leavings as she went.

I had my own work to do on that afternoon, the putting together of child and parents. I had only known my future husband as an isolated phenomenon and yet, here they were, parents in the wings, suddenly given back their child and with him, me.

They confronted this "fait accompli" with growing concern. I could see an uneasiness, a question or two in their raised eyebrows, their lengthening noses, the agitation expressed in his mother's shaking hands. I was of another background. I was young. Was I the wife for their son? He might have married a girl called Sonja who played the piano beautifully. And while they hadn't approved of her at the time, maybe they had made a mistake.... After a silence that seemed endless to me, the mother began to try again.

"Benjamin tells me you went to college."

"I graduated from Barnard."

"That's nice. And what did you study there?"

"I was an English major."

"Oh really! I read a lot myself."

"My mother reads the Russians, in the original."

"Yes, I like Pushkin the best."

Unfortunately, I had never read Pushkin. In fact, I was quite ignorant of Russian literature, save for *Crime and Punishment*. Still, the mother's spirits improved. The father's too. They would now tell me about the man I was going to marry. Did I know that he was given to hay fever, his mother asked. I acknowledged that I did not. And that he was especially allergic to dust. They hoped that I did not favor down pillows as sponge rubber would be best. Sponge rubber would be satisfactory, I said. Would I see that he took his injections in the spring? I could. As my answers were satisfactory, they opened up and in the end, I learned that Benjamin had sung *The Marriage of Figaro* at an early age, that his memory was extraordinary. Also, that he was skilled in argument, that he could argue with anybody about their politics and win. I could see that it was at home that he had sharpened his stock-in-trade, his gift for argument on which I knew he had won perfect scores, then scholarships, degrees, a position with a bank, the history of modern Europe notwithstanding.

And what were my politics, his father wished to know. He was pleased enough that I didn't have any. Politics could pose difficulty, even danger. Were they themselves not implicated in the fifties, as well as their son? And what had they gained by it? Severe headaches. Indigestion when there had never been difficulty before. Politics were better read about in the paper. With this question settled, he went on to tell now about Benjamin's work and how it should always come first. Of course, he needed absolute quiet when he was concentrating. Benjamin was to have a career and, of course, his wife should help. Did I think I could provide such an atmosphere for his son? During the conversation, Benjamin took refuge in the newspaper, walked about, stopped at the bookcase in the hall, rifled through the papers in a drawer. But, as he was always in sight of me, I knew that he was listening and that an uneasiness was subsiding.

On a gray monogrammed damask which now covered the white porcelain-topped table were arranged hot borscht, a pudding made of beans. Crystal and flatware sparkled as did surfaces designed for work. All was polished from use but for scratches, little dull patches from repeated scrubbings of bowl or plate or counter.

I tried to return to the Russians. Had the mother read *Crime and Punishment,* I wondered. She had not. She heard very bad things about the author, in fact. Did I know he was a gambler, she remarked, and that he had perhaps himself committed crimes? How else did he come to write about such things, and she looked me over as if I myself might be the criminal. I thought it best to mention another safer author. Did she think Tolstoy a great stylist? Did I not know he had gone off and left his wife! I felt personally rebuked, my morals suspect.

Looking at the others, I saw they were content to be silent while they ate. . . . I, too, fell silent. From time to time, there would come queries in my direction. Did I like the pudding, his father wished to know. I did. I thought it was wonderful. Would I like a second helping, he then asked. I couldn't. Thank you. "And why not?" his mother demanded. "There's plenty more in the refrigerator!" And the door swung open to reveal that there were indeed more plastic-covered bowls of the sort that stood in relief on the counter directly to my back. I tried to do as well as I could by my dinner to recover in some measure from the displeasure I incurred.

After the meal, we returned to the living room. I took a closer look at the surroundings, which were quite bare save for couch and chair and in the corner a radio cabinet, hollow, gaping; not a picture, only a poor plant in a china elephant and wheelbarrow. The windows were curtainless. Nor could venetian blinds at half-angle conceal the drab treeless courtyard which was their view. On my way to the bathroom, I observed the framed diplomas and a graduation photo of a younger Benjamin. These were their decorations.

The afternoon wore on and still we stayed. It was not for me to say we should be going. I looked at Benjamin. He looked down at his hands. We continued to sit. Finally, his parents stood up.

Walking back to the subway, I felt that I had been let out of some terrible fate. Not that I had been treated badly, rather I had been subject, by virtue of my compliance, to the alien will of this graying pair, well intentioned as they seemed to someone of what had been termed earlier in our conversation, "another background." The food, the drink, the motion of the train going uptown lulled me into another life, ageless, feminine, composed of the undigestible elements of this encounter. Call it a dream or a fantasy or perhaps an act of sympathy.

I was awakened by a great noise below my window, trashmen coming to take the barrels away, barrels and barrels, for the house I lived in was very large and there were many other lives within. I propped my head in such a way as to be able to watch their movements. Each man had on his back a kind of harness into which the barrel could fit, making somewhat easier the task, the lifting, the carrying between courtyard and street, where their great truck received the contents of these barrels. I did not like to think about what was in them though I knew in fact something of their contents. Did I not see my own father carry away each bag as it was full from underneath the sink! So sour the smell, so unpleasant the handling, my own mother took no part in its removal. I understood, therefore, that it was men's work. And I watched the men below me as I watched my own father within, seeing in the work, the ease with which it was done, the repetition too, a kind of beauty. I could tell that the work was good though what was worked with, the barrels, their contents, might reek of foul smells, filled as they were with what could not be eaten.

In the kitchen, the water is running, full-pressured, strong. Now the pounding begins. My mother is particular that not a pocket of air be there before she cuts the dough into strips and arranges it in the pan, or so I conclude from this distance, for I have never actually seen the process. I see her return to her room to dress. Her dress is flour-stained as are her hands and face. She does not look at me as she goes by.

I hear slippers flapping. It is my father, the worldly one, getting his paper. He pauses, glancing at the print, and returns wordless to his room. His hair, full, bushy

56

despite his years, touches the arch at the center and he is gone.

The courtyard below my window is empty save for the pigeons. I do not mind their sound, throaty, sweet, more like a murmur than a call, telling me it's time to get up. To move is an exertion as if I were hampered in some way but am not. There! And now to braid my hair, heavy, long, stopping between the plaits to gather strength.

They say I am not fit to go outside and that I must stay here with them. I am small for my years and do not have as much strength as I need. So my mother tells me, and I know her to be right as I am tired nearly all the time. I am tired now but cannot take overlong, not wanting to resist. I did resist him once, won't again. . . . We were at the table in the kitchen. My father's seat allows the best view. Whereas I have to lean forward to see out.

It was in the evening, a time I am wont to feel the difficulty of life, that I remarked on the size of my portion. I wanted more. My father refused me. Reaching across the table, I took his meat. His eyes grew large in his head, his mouth twisted with rage. But before his hand could reach me, for that I could see was his intention, I got out of my seat and ran toward the outside door. The handle turned, but the door wouldn't open. Why had I ever thought it would! I made one final effort to get out, and threw myself against the door. And he was there, shaking me until my bones rattled.

I awoke to my mother bending over me, though

where my father had gone I didn't know. Perhaps, he was in another part of the house. Perhaps, he had gone away. I can't remember now. All I knew was that I was glad he was gone and I could continue to lie there. .... I didn't think I could get up. Indeed, I didn't get up for days. Nor did I see him, in all that time. And when at last my life took its usual course, I had changed. Never again did I seek to incur the wrath of my father or the sorrow of my mother.

I think my mother felt that it was her fault.

Returned from this imaginative voyage, I looked up at Benjamin beside me on the train. I felt moved as I had never been. I felt I had been inside his life and could understand why he little spoke of it. To his silence walking back to my apartment, I attributed great feeling. And I thought with a kind of joy, This is the man I am going to marry.

"Madame, est-ce que je peux avoir encore du café?" Why will you be so slow with the coffee, Madame?

4

The Ansonia Residential Hotel

Outside the quadrangle in that part of town where Benjamin lived in the days when we were courting, was a row of fraternity houses. These had little to do with the nonresident independents who came to the university with the single-minded purpose of completing their degrees. Farther down on that particular street, away from Broadway and the noise, where, as it turned out, such students lived, among the transient and the aging, I looked for the Ansonia Residential Hotel. It was not to be found. I was looking for a sign. I saw only fire escapes zigzagging up the dull brick tenements which cried out to be leveled for the depression that was in them. I was about to turn back, when Benjamin appeared from around the corner at the Broadway end of the street.

"I'm sorry I'm late. I lost track of the time. I was working over a section of the thesis."

"I'm glad you're here. I was just about to turn back." What if I had turned back? Would he have come after me? Perhaps there would have been relief on two sides.

The marquee, short the bulbs to announce itself, called attention to the rundown state of the hotel as did the five-and-dime window shades, which were ragged at the edges. I could see they had never been replaced. Once off-white, their color was nearer to parchment.

"Which is your room?" I asked.

"That one!"

Benjamin pointed to the double-hung windows in front of which was a railing and a deep cement area where there was trash, boxes of old clothes which had been picked through, an old lamp whose wire was frayed, a torn lampshade, broken glass, an assortment of what looked like medicine bottles.

"You left the light on," I offered. It was all that I could do to speak, I was so put off by the surroundings.

"I thought we'd go in," said Benjamin, urging me with a gentle nudging of my arm....We had been to the movies and on another afternoon had walked to the New York Public Library. That was when the weather was warm. I took off my shoes, which were making me miserable. A blister had formed on the outside of my big toe. And the heels were making me tip forward as I walked. It felt so much better I did not mind how black my feet were turning. "Are you sure we shouldn't hop a bus?" asked Benjamin. But I didn't want to give up. I felt strangely light continuing, as if by taking off my shoes I had again become the child. Or was it Benjamin who was having this effect on me?

In the evening, as the light was fading from the sky, we went back up Broadway to a concert at Julliard, stopping off to eat along the way. It was Benjamin who had gotten the tickets; I was ready to go home, weariness overcoming me after the long walk and the high spirits of the afternoon. But I went, anxious to please Benjamin. "The pianist is a friend," Benjamin explained, letting me know the evening was special.

To myself, I wondered what sort of friend I would be meeting. I had yet to meet any of Benjamin's friends. I did not expect the pianist would be a girl. The concert itself was eclipsed, shut out, by this unhappy revelation. What sort of friend has she been, I wondered, and on what terms did they see each other? To make matters worse, the girl was pretty, though she was taller than myself and somewhat older. The color of her skin was nut brown like no one I'd ever known. Was she Sephardic or could she be Armenian? I took a look at the program notes to see what I could learn about the girl. She had been to Hunter. She had graduated from Julliard. It mentioned who her teachers were and that she had won a contest, which wasn't much to remark upon. Nowhere did it say that she was married. Wasn't she interested in marriage? What about Benjamin? I couldn't wait for the wretched piece to end.

"Did you go out with her?" I asked. And I sensed welling up in me a violent case of jealousy, which made me want to lay my claim on Benjamin.

The lights were dimming, and we had to rush back to

our seats. But an understanding had been reached, our relationship was deepening.

"Shall we go inside?" asked Benjamin. "You seem to hesitate."

"Do I?" I answered him. "I didn't mean to." And I walked in the direction of his front door. The night was cold. I felt the chill in me. And not the warm sweater underneath or the black fur-trimmed coat I wore in those days, could keep it out.

I stood on the stairs behind Benjamin while he searched through the outside pockets of his overcoat, the jacket underneath, and finally into his pants' pocket for the key that would allow us to enter unobserved.

"It must be somewhere," said Benjamin.

He became rattled by the search, turning his pockets out, so that papers and wallet dropped onto the stoop and finally the missing key. All this difficulty did not allay my own anxiety, which was mounting now. I wanted out and wracked my brains to think of how it could be managed. I would have given anything to have been elsewhere, and yet, when the door opened, I followed him in.

I'd been to other rooming houses and smelled their smells—dirty laundry, sour milk stinking from neglect in the refrigerator, leftovers that should have been thrown out, an unsuccessful casserole that no one wanted to eat. I was thinking of Harvey, whom I had met at a fraternity dance. He was also interested in marriage. I let him take me out any number of times. I liked to receive his telephone calls, which invariably came rather late at night, just as I was getting comfortable in my bed. I enjoyed those talks. Yet I left him one night in his doorway without so much as a regret.

"You'll never get anyone," he called after me, "cock teaser!"

I thought I had made myself perfectly clear. Harvey was planning to go to medical school. I had no intentions of waiting for him.

On our left as Benjamin and I entered I saw a kitchen which was spotless. Farther down the hall, opened to us through an archway, was a very small sitting room with walls that were finished in craftex, something my own mother would never have stood. How well I remember when our apartment had been sandblasted, the walls canvased and painted a delicate French blue.

"Damn," said Benjamin, who was irritated that his precautions had now proven unnecessary. On an old-fashioned settee and side chairs covered in a faded floral pattern sat two women in housedresses and a man in trousers, overlarge, suspenders made of leather to hold them up, long underwear underneath. They were grinning at us. As we passed, I nodded and smiled. Encouraged, they nodded and smiled back at me. "How do you do, miss," an old woman said. When I no longer could see them, I could still feel them sinking back into their chairs, once more returned to their private worlds. And it was then I came in touch with a repugnance, a drawing back from the persons and the place. But then I thought, perhaps he doesn't mind, perhaps it's only me and I am less therefore. For I was ready to be converted from a guilty creature of comfort and corruption, spoiled by parents eager to do well by their daughter, to what I thought I ought to become, by way of penance perhaps, which was definitely someone purer, whose judgments might proceed from values less material. This sense of myself may have been communicated to me by a father who himself had known what it was like to go without. But becoming successful, he felt his poverty had done him good. And that his daughter, with all that he had given her, could not possibly do as well as himself, certainly not as well as her mother, who had replaced his own mother as the being most necessary to him. As he was my father, I had come to believe that he was right.

"How did you ever find this place?" I asked Benjamin, wanting him to tell me all he could. Benjamin, overcome still by the entrance we made—he did, after all, live with these people—motioned to me to be silent. It was only when the door of his room was shut, that he was willing to give me an answer.

"It's near the library," he said.

Before I could monitor my response, it came out:

"But the smell," I demanded, "how can you bear the smell!"

"I don't know what smell you mean!" responded Benjamin. "What are you talking about?" And I thought, He doesn't smell it, the memory of which or the smell itself that was with me still. And then it came to me what the smell was and I could name it.

"It's the smell of old people. They're all old in this place!"

"Well, so what if they are?" answered Benjamin, turning on me now. "If I had your money, do you think I'd be living here?" I was humbled. For, of course, I remembered that he was as my own father had been, a poor student, unsupported by parents at home. And I felt the contrast between us entirely to my disfavor. Whatever I was, was based on that which had been given, which I never could forget. Reduced by the meanness of my reaction, I was eager to show I could improve. What better fate to choose than this ultimate offer to one who, by his own efforts, was establishing himself in a career? I threw myself into his arms and attempted to discover there a passion. Pleased with me now, and more confident, he offered me a familiar sort of pat.

"I'll be right back," he said.

When he had gone, I took a good look at the room. In the corner, angled into the room, stood an iron bedstead with a night table beside it. The nubby white bedspread had been neatly turned down. Nothing was out of place, not the papers on the desk in front of the windows I had wanted to see into nor the books piled on the reading chair to the side of it, oatmeal-covered, mahogany-armed. Was he always this neat? I wanted to know. Neatness was not a quality I had cultivated.

The chest of drawers, I remember, was of the sort you see in secondhand stores with no pretention to antiquity, machine-carved with brass teardrop pulls the color of bullets. The floral-patterned linoleum was cracked in places and coming away from its backing. On the wall, crooked above the bed, the Holy Virgin looked down on me. Why hadn't he put the thing away? But then I reminded myself that perhaps this was not of any consequence either, and went unnoticed therefore. I got off my clothes in a hurry, I wanted to be in the bed when he got back and I took to the cold and mended covers for my protection. I felt a need, too near the surface to put down, to find under the covers my way out.

Benjamin returned from the bathroom with an expression decidedly serious, grim, in fact, but he smiled when he saw me in the bed. He had thought I would be difficult? But whatever for? I was willing. Had he not won all the prizes? Was he not the beneficiary of a first-rate education, early publications, a career which was promising, and now me!

Giving me his back, he removed his trousers, folding them onto the chair; shirt, tie and jacket quickly followed. I had never seen Benjamin, nor did it occur to me what his body would be like. It was his high-sounding morals that had attracted me, proof of which had appeared in article form in a magazine called *Money* and another in *Review*. But his body was better, leaner, harder than I anticipated. So far so good, though I noticed he left on his underwear, which I felt was unfair, when I experienced my own goose-covered flesh against the sheets.

The act itself, for what it was worth, was quickly done: "Move," said Benjamin, and I moved, conscientious to a fault. And with a fair amount of effort, the deed was done.

In the morning, I studied my face in the mirror. What I saw was a young woman unaffected in all the outward signs, no horns, no hardened look. Then it was possible to regard such an encounter as a devastation of everything one had stood for, or, as an initiation into the mysteries of life. But perhaps, it takes longer, I reflected, and hurried back to a waiting Benjamin.

We did not see each other for several days during which time I went through a succession of miserable feelings. Was it commitment? Responsibility? The reaction was panic.

The subject of marriage did come up at our very next meeting. Benjamin had mentioned taking a job with a New York bank. He was interested in power. In our society, money is power, he had said. One must use it. He looked forward to using several billions, in fact. Since I had seen him, he had been offered a post in the Paris branch, which put the most favorable construction on his position. In Paris, spending would be more appealing. But it put a pressure on us with regard to time. We would marry, of course. And sooner than I would have planned.

"I'll get the tickets this week," said Benjamin.

"What about waiting until the end of the month?"

Was it necessary to be in that much of a hurry?

"The end of the month," said Benjamin, "why, they'll be all sold out!"

"Do you think so?"

As Benjamin was pressing for a resolution to our arrangements, I agreed. Though alone in my room that night, unable to sleep, sensitive to noises, the ambulances and police sirens, the chiming of the church bells on the hour, I was tempted to go back on my word. What if I changed my mind? The institution like death itself might never be undone.

I had an impulse to bolt. But whether from lack of courage or fundamental ease in the projected arrangement deeper than mere disinclination, I went ahead. Clearly, I was not to be modified by the unsuitability of marriage to Benjamin. Nor by an inability to imagine myself a wife and mother. For I regret to say that nothing had happened to modify the dread of the swelling up, the delivery itself, certainly not relations with Benjamin.

5

Return Match

I sat in the lobby of my building, it was two weeks before we were to go, waiting for Benjamin, taking comfort in the notion that my misery was not unusual. Brides were often miserable. It was the contract, not Benjamin, that got me down. Furthermore, no one I knew had been married, only parents who, with their bourgeois lifestyle, were not to be looked to as models. Could people who played bridge be my models? Or worse, belonged to country clubs! For, of course, I thought of myself as Bohemian.

"When you're married, it will be easier," a friend had said. I had sat up with her on the Saturday before and gone over the decision, trying to think of alternatives, none of which seemed right. "It's a case of nerves," said Alice, "otherwise, you would certainly have decided to

leave him. You don't have to get married," she had said.
"Do you?" Of course, I did not.

Alice was going off to Italy to study art. This she had
announced to me on Monday, having on her own applied for a national grant. Alice, with the long dark hair
and rumpled skirts, who used to share a cubicle in the
basement of the library. I wrote to her from Paris. I
might have met her there. She said she would be coming. . . . We had arranged to meet before her departure,
underneath the arch in Washington Square. I had been
uptown and lost track of the time. Frantic, I arrived an
hour late. Of course, she was gone. I walked around the
Village to see if I could find her. I went down to
Bleecker Street to the Café Rienzi. I asked the waiter
if he had seen her. The place was empty, only the chess
players continued relentless at their game. I gave him a
very good description. She had been there, he said, she
had not left a message. Yes, he was sure it was the girl.
She never gave me her address at home. So I wrote
American Express. I never did get an answer.

I looked to see if Benjamin was coming. But I saw
only our doorman, Manuel, from Puerto Rico, who was
working so that his family could come and join him, a
mother and five sisters, he had said. Five sisters was a
lot, I had commented, thinking it might be nice to be
one of five with a brother who was working to bring one
along into a future which would be assured.

The thought occurred to me that perhaps Benjamin
had had second thoughts! Could he have gone back to
his pianist instead? Finally, he appeared. He had been

running, an appointment had detained him, the buses would not stop, and he had had to walk all the way from the other side of the park. His color was good. Normally, his skin was quite pale. City pallor was what my mother called it. I think she thought that the people who had it should do something about it, for the sake of others like herself. It spoke of bad habits, she said, and required that one take trips, as she did, or try to get more sleep. Vitamins might also be of help.

"Sorry I'm late," said Benjamin. "Are you all right? You look terrible."

"I thought you weren't going to come."

"That's ridiculous! I said I was coming, didn't I?"

I told Benjamin a little about my mother. I wanted to prepare him. Or did I think to find an ally? We had quarreled, my mother and I. She wanted to know why wouldn't I come with her to one of the benefits. I said I didn't want to go. That wasn't a reason, she answered. "You ought to come for my sake," she concluded. "Your sake," said I. "But what about me?" Which was always a question when I was young. That Benjamin would like her, that they would in fact get on, had never occurred to me. Had he not spoken at great length about easy money, how it destroyed ambition, character, even among the Jews who were in danger of losing their edge!

"In New York?" I asked.

"Even here," he had said with absolute conviction. "Soon, they will be replaced by the blacks and the Puerto Ricans."

I trembled before the severity of Benjamin's views and felt myself to be an instance of the corruption he had been describing. Lack of expectations, an easy life, had taken me over and not a jot of ambition coursed through my veins, save to marry, which was less an ambition than an inevitability. As to what life would bring me in the future, I had only the vaguest of notions. Not to disgrace myself would in some measure be enough. There was that tendency in me, dark and rebellious, which reminded my mother of her elder sister whose life she characterized as "wasted." Antoinette, or "poor Antoinette" as she was called, had relieved her family by an early death. Self-neglect was the verdict, I remember hearing, the particular form of it, staying in bed, reading cheap novels, when she might have been working instead. Or better still married; a single woman was no use at all, my mother said.

Ideas about what to do with my own life gave out beyond college. Call it a lack of imagination, if you will. It was not until the move to Paris that I thought of a career. Only then did I discover a need to fill my days. Benjamin, on the other hand, looked ahead and saw in a career a chance to show his mettle. I think he enjoyed the idea of his advancement. This difference between us appealed. For I counted not a little on such determination to get me through my life.

"So," said my mother, "this is Benjamin." And she took his hands and held them out from her, so that she might see him to advantage.

"Well now," said my mother, "tell me all about yourself, Benjamin."

"Where shall I begin?"

"Why at the beginning, of course."

While they talked, I was distracted by the look of the apartment. I noticed, for example, that the upholstery was fading. I remembered when it was new. It was an anniversary, their twenty-fifth, I think. They had had a party. A bar was set up in the dining room, the furniture moved out, coat racks to the right and left as you came in the front door. Trays of hors d'oeuvres were brought in by the kitchen entrance, arriving hot on silver trays that were passed round by waiters who looked familiar. There was dancing. My father asked me to do the tango. I had trouble managing such difficult steps. He tried to be patient. "This is how to do it," he said. "One two, one two three four." I improved a little and we continued, he counting all the while, until my mother cut in. I stood to the side. Glad to be out of it, I watched. The tempo shifted to a waltz, one two three, one two three, and they whirled past me. They were a pretty pair, my mother in pale green chiffon, her skirts flying. He was Fred Astaire, a little shorter, perhaps, and slightly overweight.

And when the music stopped, I was introduced to their friends.

"This is Anna. Have you met our Anna?"

Looking at my mother, I noticed that her make-up was more marked, the sharpness of her cheekbones more evident. And her nose, never long before now, seemed so. And I felt a softening toward her, but not for long. For I listened to her conversation and was critical. She had come back from another trip. I had heard it before. Her descriptions had always been post-card pictures of islands and hotel rooms. I sought out an opportunity to wander up to my old bedroom, stopping to look at the photographs above a table, taken in the early part of the century. Grandparents who appear dignified, he handsome, she bosomy, looking like my own father round the eyes, with hair pulled tight into a bun, rather like my own. Beside them, their son, my father's eldest brother, dead in a war which filtered through to me in talk. And I as a consequence crawled across its battlefields in dreams. In the newsreels, where I was taken by my father on Saturdays, I got other violent images to store away which pop up even now from time to time.

"Anna, Anna, where are you? Come downstairs, we're looking at photographs. Here's Anna as a child. Wasn't she beautiful? Wherever she went people couldn't do enough for her. Headwaiters gave her the flower arrangements, didn't they darling?" And I nod knowing that if I don't she'll ask again, "Whatever happened Anna?"

I grew up, as do we all, mother. . . . I look at the picture of a little girl with pail and shovel under an umbrella, which stands as a fragile reminder to parental concern. Under those stripes, whole civilizations were dug out with roads winding up mountains, cars and people formed of gathered sticks.

"You won't have to take care of Anna anymore, Mrs.

Spring," said Benjamin, leaning over to reach for my hand, "she's my responsibility now."

And we went into the dining room for lunch, chicken and peas, watercress to the side, not so much as to cover the plate. My mother was always very fond of china, so much so that to this day I notice a pretty place setting for her sake while I myself have always preferred to eat on pottery.

That day, as I eyed the flatware and the crystal, I had to stop myself coveting it, knowing too well that what I really wanted was not the objects but her death. And so I spread out the napkin and ate my portion in silence.

6

Leave-taking

Here's another picture. The stiffness of it, its cracks down the middle and sides curling away from their backing are as scars imperfectly grown together. Healing is out of the question; instamatic inefficiency is disposing of itself. The box which catches it is held by the person who is not seen, a Mrs. Clara Spring. She is one of two missing from the grouping. The other is a young man of about twenty-nine years, her son-in-law at the time of this telling, which is later, quite a few years later, in fact. He is seeing to the baggage and has already been gone for some time. Three are being photographed, Mr. and Mrs. Small, parents of the groom who, but for their son, would never have been photographed with such a girl . . . younger than she should be, dressed in a jacket, mittens, not gloves, and flats. She is pretty in a wistful sort of way, though not at all the wife for their Benjamin.

The ceremony was performed yesterday at City Hall. At least it was in Brooklyn so they had something their way. The time was not convenient for the Smalls. And they did not like the choice of restaurant where they went later, after the marriage had been performed. They didn't like the menu, either, which was filet mignon. There might have been a choice! Why hadn't they been consulted, they wanted to know! They had addressed their complaints to the girl who couldn't answer them. They had asked Benjamin. But he had said it wasn't any of their business. And as to the date of the ceremony, they believed it was inconvenient. Uncle Charlie couldn't come. He was in Cleveland on that day. And what about their cousin Isidor? Couldn't they have gotten married the day before? There is much more that could be said by way of a complaint. But why should they be listened to anyway!

Now they are on the pier waiting.

"Where's Benjamin?" It is Mr. Small who is speaking to the daughter-in-law.

"What takes him so long?" asks Mrs. Small.

Her face is pinched; her eyes are full, blinking back the years. This is part of another picture which is unrecorded here. In this picture, the husband is touching the arm of the little woman, the wife and the life. This is how he feels, about her. It's all in the picture, how they think the girl is linked to the source of the pain. See the stiffness of their bodies that they be next to her, that it be the three of them and the other, the girl's mother, who is taking the picture! All has been ultimately recorded in a catalogue of injuries not to be forgotten. Certainly not by them. And what of the girl? Anna, she is the young one in the photograph, also remembers. She is a cracked pot at bottom, emptied out, what is left is ... but that is part of another picture. Turned slightly, Anna falls in shadow. But the graying pair appear long-faced in their history, which they wear proudly. They do not want pity. They want us to share in the wearing of their mantle of miseries, or better, do homage, tell their story, that in another life they saved scraps and suet, made garments to wear and broth to drink which could neither cover nor fill them. Heavy the days, carrying stones off the ground on which they leaned, looking out, turning fat to tallow to tote in a cart to market. It was their business to make candles. And the land changed hands, now Russian, now not, never theirs, one time too many to tighten the belt. . . . So it was that Mr. and Mrs. Small came to America.

But! thinks the one who is in shadow, to be a martyr to such a history is something! You can use it!

What can Anna use? This is not clear yet. Not her skin crackling like crumpled newsprint round eyelids which are closing now for the take.

"Now this time, keep your eyes open everyone!" It is the photographer who is urging her subjects on. Born in America, as were mother and grandmother before her, Mrs. Clara Spring speaks quite distinctly. Speech is very important to her. It was Miss Blanchard, a friendly third grade teacher, who had criticized her own sibilants, all those many years ago, and she had taken this criticism to heart, correcting the offending s's and z's as best she could. And Anna benefited from her own good example: "Say cheese everyone!"

Mr. and Mrs. Small and the daughter-in-law try to smile into the eye of her camera but they have trouble. Mrs. Small feels as if her smile has been pasted on. Her husband will not pretend to bother. Why should he smile to please the officious and pushy Mrs. Spring? He'll not even call her by her first name, if he can help it. Of course, he doesn't want an out-and-out brawl.

"This is your last chance everyone!" There is a cheerfulness about the woman which is running counter to the spirit of the group being photographed, all of whom must again go through the motions of being good subjects. Anna and Mrs. Small make an effort to go along with her, but they fail.

"Well, I suppose this will just have to do," concedes Mrs. Spring to the reluctant group she is trying to photograph. She is most put out by Anna, her own daughter, who is being uncooperative as usual. "I don't know why you couldn't have looked more alive!" she says.

Mrs. Spring is turning full-face to Anna, letting the parentlike posture have its effect. Anna slides off as is her way, choosing not to take it up that she be in shadow out of spite. She doesn't want to take her mother on today. It is already too much. She looks forward to this being over, when she will have lived through this terrible day.

Left without her opposition, Mrs. Spring takes another tack. Being aware that she also is on view, she enters, therefore, the group, putting her arm round the object of her displeasure. It is not the first time she has been at odds with her difficult daughter. It is an old story, going back to when Anna was a child. She was obstinate, always thinking she should have her own way. In particular, there was the matter of the summer house, Anna insisting that they should keep it. That was after Joseph's death. And it was too much for her. Anna ought to have known that! But she couldn't accept no for an answer. So she had practically to force her difficult daughter to go to camp. Anna thought it was a punishment, which it wasn't. Anyone should know that! It cost a lot of money to send a child to camp.

"I know you'll want to have these!" says Mrs. Spring, handing the not yet dry photographs to the already miserable parents of her daughter's new husband.

"We'd like the picture of our son," asserts the father, the color high now in his cossack cheeks. Mrs. Small touches his arm, reminding him that it will be over soon and they need not have more to do with the mother of their son's wife, a queer managing person as far as she's concerned. But then what do you expect from such a choice! How she should have loved to have an in-law like her own dear Minna whom she did not get to see enough since she moved to Coney Island for her health.

Though they did drive out there sometimes, in the summer, when the weather got hot, taking the air, walking sometimes clear to the end of the boardwalk, stopping for an ice cream along the way, resting when they were tired on a bench, getting back late, having such a nice time.

The photographer is now disinclined to continue and puts away her equipment, folding the camera back into its case. "There!" She'll not do more! They cannot fault her in what she does, can they? Her own daughter has become a difficult subject. But these in-laws are worse! Not that it is surprising. Hardly. She might have expected as much, adding insult to injury. Is this what she raised her for? Such an alliance can only breed trouble, which she had tried to tell Anna. But no. She wouldn't listen to her mother. Never mind. It won't be her struggle after today. Far better to take photographs than to go on standing here grimly as some are, making out that what is happening is a tragedy.

On Mrs. Spring's arm is a shopping bag from Bergdorf's. Having been out the day before yesterday, she remembered to buy a going-away gift. And the commotion was terrible on the Saturday before Easter. But she braved it all to do right by her Anna, standing in line for the salesgirl. Which was not why she went to shop at Bergdorf's. She might have been at Klein's on the Square or Macy's! Even when she went to the ladies' room, she had had to wait. But she got a new handbag for Anna. The old one was worn out, and her shoes! Mrs. Spring looks down at Anna's footgear, scruffy as usual. She never had been able to do anything with the girl.

"This is for you, darling."

Without looking, Anna knows what is in the package. Pocketbooks are a favorite of her mother's. Rows of pocketbooks peek out at her when opening the closet door. Well, let her have it her own way today.

"Make it last!" says Anna's mother, thinking, She'll not get another. Mrs. Spring's done buying her daughter clothes. Which is fine with Anna who by the time of this leave-taking has had enough of gifts implying a criticism or a judgment. Anna remembers now what her mother said of one of her own sister's gifts. "She must have won it in a bridge game," hurt that the gift demonstrated lack of care. I wonder why she bothers at all! would be her feeling, which is what her own daughter was feeling at the moment.

"And here's a little something for Benjamin!" Mrs. Spring had had so much to think about she almost forgot her new son-in-law, but there, in the cabinet in the dining room, she discovered an unopened bottle. The perfect gift for Benjamin!

Mrs. Spring looks in vain toward the Smalls for their approval.

"Shall I open it?" Anna asks. The silence is becoming painful.

"Don't bother dear. It's a bottle of slivovitz. I was sure Benjamin would like slivovitz. Does he Anna?"

Again Mrs. Spring turns toward those she would have on her side. Whatever their differences, they are all parents. Aren't they? Never mind where they were born or what their style of life is, about which she has a pretty good idea. In her childhood, she had known people just off the boat.

Mr. and Mrs. Small are now speaking between themselves, concern is mounting. Where is their son? What does his protracted absence mean? Could he be sick? Has something gone wrong! They remember when he was to have been at dinner at their house. He had been coming from upstate New York, where he had been visiting friends who lived in the country, that nice young couple who lived in the gardener's cottage on the Zubriskie Estate. It was not that they didn't know where he was coming from, but that they expected him at three. At four o'clock, he hadn't arrived or called. They knew what had to be done. They had had to eat the dinner and put away what was for Benjamin, which was really too bad as they had gone to so much trouble, and call the police departments, each and every one of them along the way. But that he isn't on some highway is small comfort today, for they know that where he should be is with them.

Meanwhile, mother and daughter are left to their own devices. Mrs. Spring would like to cut it short, which she communicates by gesture to her daughter, head angling toward the exit, eyeballs too. She cannot speak; the in-laws might hear her. Not about a matter like that. Above all, she doesn't want to hurt their feelings. She, at least, will have been considerate!

Anna, wishing her mother would stay longer . . . the

fact of her leaving is coming home to her ... turns into the crowd of heads for the one that she is looking for. He is not to be found. He is not coming toward her to stop her mother from leaving her. Far better to be there already, an ocean between, sending her mother a telegram, JUST MARRIED, WISH YOU COULD HAVE BEEN HERE. SEND BELONGINGS. She had talked about the matter to Benjamin. It would hurt them all too much, he had said. But what about Anna?

Too late! Mrs. Spring is in motion.

"Good-bye, darling, write often!" And her mother touches the cheeks and forehead of her child, that Anna came of her womb is remembered in her taking leave. And the daughter is taken into her mother's arms, where she gets the feeling of skin, scented, strong. Anna is now in a field of brown-speckled flesh and heavy hair. But not for long. For above the heads of the crowd are arms waving and the one she is looking for. It is Benjamin, who can now tell her where he's been!

"They didn't have our names on the passenger list! These damn bureaucracies are stupid and unnecessary!"

But why must he just now change the world, with his arguments? She has been needing him.

His own mother is bewildered by his talk. She can't make out his explanation. It's hard for her to hear. He tells her again of the trouble he's been having. But she doesn't understand. She is shaking her head, her eyes are filling with tears. Why isn't she to Benjamin what she was? What has happened to them? What are these explanations to her who will be missing him? He who has been, for so many years, her whole life! What will be left?

And his father embracing him remembers his own past and thinks that to go is masculine, to be left isn't. He also has left a country, parents who had expectations of him, his sister, two half brothers by his father's second marriage, who he's never seen since and their letters come rarely. He'll try to explain it to his wife, later, when they're back in their kitchen on Pitkin Avenue. How many cups of tea they have sipped together working out the past. His wife, who was a good mother, will recall their Benjie in short pants with a matching jacket, made specially for him by the tailor who came from the Ukraine, not from the same village as himself, but close. And they'll speak of the others who were sitting with them, aunts and uncles, cousins, the lady downstairs who moved to Florida and the husband who died of a heart attack. Hadn't he told their neighbor that the way he worked was a madness especially in the country where everyone knows you're supposed to rest! They will remember all of them who were with them when they were watching their Benjamin reciting so beautifully, "Ich ben a Yid."

"Take care of yourself, son. Be sure to write once a week. You know how your mother is!"

They both understand how his mother, with her concerns and her ailments, her back and her legs, the rest she needed to take care of them, always was looking toward her son! Benjamin, child of his mother's dreams, from whom all that is good in a disappointing world must forever come, will have to continue to carry his burden an ocean away where perhaps it will be easier.

Mrs. Small takes a step back. It is time. Anna has a last look at her mother who, wearing a black suit and hat, wide-brimmed, shading skin which is aging and eyes faded but smart, darting about, blue, evasive, rushes in for a final embrace.

"Good-bye, darling. Take care of yourself."

"You too, Mother."

All passengers begin to move toward the ramp and the parents come too.

"Can a job be so important?" Mrs. Small cries out, her voice high above the others.

"You know we've gone through this. It's too late," answers Benjamin back.

"Let him go, Mother!" Mr. Small turns her in the direction they will be going. And the crowd comes up between them and their departing son.

Anna catches sight of her own mother's back.

"It's the opportunity of a lifetime!" shouts Benjamin. Can his mother hear him?

"Isn't America good enough?" This his mother flings at him through tears, uncontrollable now. All that they did for him! Piano lessons. Orthodontia. Camp. What did it mean?

Benjamin breaks through the crowd finally to catch his mother in his arms. Does she want him to give it all up? Never was she satisfied, always wanting more, his diplomas and his prizes and now this!

"I'll write to you, we'll visit. You'll see. It'll be all right, better than ever before." What else can he say to her? What else does she want? He's no longer a kid. He has a wife, responsibilities.

Mr. Small steps in, embraces his son, and the departure is in motion.

7

Shipboard

Orange peels in the wake, bottles and bags, seabirds
swoop down, heron and waterfowl, piper and gull.
Anna Spring now Small looks and is attracted to the
sight. She thinks then on debris, recently having been to
see her parents-in-law who, their old life having crum-
bled, were intent, in manner and logistics, to separate
out from neighbors, from the street, the smells within, a
broken-down elevator now trash bin, overflowing, and
outside the old tires, a mattress, rat-infested stuffing
partly out, and there, to the side of the level part before
the descent downward to the place where they came out
of the el, an abandoned car, stripped, skeletal, and on
the one side a vast garage or body shop reaching inside
and under one of the abandoned tenements.

Entering by the side of it, Anna and Benjamin met a

new neighbor, new neighbors were coming in and out all the time now the neighborhood had deteriorated.

"Man, I'm moving out of here, the trash is moving in!" And it was as he described. There were piles of it on the lot that formed the corner, triangular in shape, blackened from fire, too small ever to build on. And everywhere else too. For the trashmen didn't come anymore, not a sign of them. They did their work in other parts of town.

Anna and Benjamin and the neighbor had all three of them taken the elevator together that day, the neighbor telling them what he thought of the situation.

"When it starts to go," he gestured to indicate the place and the neighborhood, "it goes quick. Where I lived before, it was the same. It sure is a shame how I have to keep moving. But I don't want to live in any junk heap!" The man pushed their floor button for them. There was no doubt about where they could be going. Only one white family was left in the building.

The elevator stopped a foot beneath the rise. She could see down the shaft. Turning up toward the man, she felt that in this strange place, she'd found a friend. He had said what it was she had been seeing. Now onto the floor, she looked up to see the bottom of the lift, his legs, and the cables waving.

"See you around," he shouted down to them.

"It's this way," said Benjamin, and he moved her toward the brown painted door. They had hardly rung when a brass plate slid back and revealed eyes looking at them.

"My mother," explained Benjamin.

Mrs. Small stood back a little, eyes rounder than before, taking in how her child looked, he seemed tired. Did he get enough sleep? But somehow she was afraid to ask him. He didn't like her to ask about his health. He said it wasn't her concern. He was tired of her always asking, which was hard for her to understand, as she was his mother, wasn't she? But Benjamin had become difficult since he went away to live. And who was this girl who was about to become her daughter-in-law? Why hadn't they met her before? Was he ashamed of her? Was he ashamed of them? What could he see in her? She wasn't a lady, of that much she was sure. Years back, hadn't she seen ladies on the avenue and she had thought, One of these days my Benjie will bring me home such a lady! Lines of concern formed round her mouth and eyes. She wanted to hide her hands, chafed from kitchen work, large-knuckled.

Mr. Small took her coat. He explained that they only had two closets. There was so much to put in them. His wife liked to save things. Anna'd be surprised how much there was in there! Sometime, they might show her treasures which they had brought with them from the other side. The girl wondered when.

Standing by the window with Anna, Mrs. Small began to speak of better times. "In the courtyard," she said, pointing through the slats of the venetian blinds, "there was a garden with zinnias, marigolds. Every year," she explained, "the old super put them in. He liked to do gardening, not like the one we have now." Mrs. Small's eyes grew vacant. She was a young mother again, down below in the courtyard with her son. He had a spade in his hand and the super was showing him how to dig. He was dressed very nicely. Perhaps he was wearing his Ukrainian shirt, the shirt her own dead mother had embroidered before she died not ever having seen the new world. He did his work from a squatting position so as not to get his clothing in the dirt. He was maybe four at the time.

"In those days," said his mother, "there was a doorman with a uniform."

Mrs. Small looked toward Anna for encouragement. Anna nodded. She certainly did wish to hear more of what the woman was saying. Satisfied, Mrs. Small continued: "He liked Benjamin. He used to play with him when he was little, didn't he Benjie?"

And Benjamin nodded and smiled, used to her asides. And she could remember the little boy that he had been to her, so difficult to talk to as he only came on Sundays, his work, this girl, all making claims on his time. . . .

Now Anna, looking down into the water from the ship, has still another vision of the parents. They are in the kitchen. It is nearing the end. They do not sit idly but busy themselves, as is their way. The father is at the sink. Slowly, he submerges each plate, raising it to the light to be inspected, sinking it into the clear water adjacent in a basin. The wife is at the table against the side wall, peeling vegetables and fruit, luscious, large. Where do they come from in this otherwise bleak scene! She separates out kinds of eatables into piles, which she arranges on unmatched saucers, the designs at the center almost gone.

The sky darkens. The old woman will not turn from her work nor the man from his, but they continue, slower, more enfeebled. To Anna, who is imagining the scene, the waiting is terrible, not to the principals, unengaged it would seem by the fact.

It comes finally as a great noise, not thunderclap but machine-produced. They are ready to begin down below. They know it is the end. The great ball and chain is sputtering and tenacious. A piece of the structure is crumbling. Already, the roof is wrenched from its underpinnings as are some of the sides. There is a shaking of the very floor they are on and a cracking. Now, an outer wall falls, window frames are first, glass splintering out in the twilight. An enveloping smoke conceals the rest.

Once again, it is clear. We see a machine approach to flatten out the ground where the structure had been and an official, preoccupied—he is taking notes—steps down from the cabin, singles out that which can be sold, iron and scrap, some reusable brick. It is a city picture.

Anna, still on the deck, looks back and sees as specks the people she has left behind; the pier is now a thin line. Pointing in the direction of the prow is the tugboat that leads them past the Battery. And there, starry-eyed as any Miss America, is that worn-out creature come to life again. . . . Once, Anna went on hot days with school friends to climb the monument from France. The climbing was endless and many times she wished she had not done it. She had no ambition, not for climbing nor for the effort that it takes making you sweat like any common laborer. It was the ride out there and back that she liked, giving her what she is having at this crossing, the stepping back, the sea sounds, out beyond the alarm clocks or telephones, intruding into the day. But the wind, they are near the ocean now, buffets them about. They stand there a little while longer, neither one of them wishing to go below into their windowless stateroom which they know will give them nothing beyond each other, two narrow berths, a john you must step up to with its corner shower stall and a toilet which makes a sucking sound, all of it made out of tin.

Never having been on an ocean liner, having only read about them or seen them on the screen, which she is learning is unreliable, made her unprepared. She sits down, uncertain what to do. She cannot sleep as her new husband begins to do, leaving Anna her book, precious little to fend off the departure. With difficulty, she gets up again, understands that the boat, the rocking, nothing to one who is used to it, is going to give her a rough crossing.

8

Getting Ready to Leave the Apartment to Go Out

Not wanting to go out, wanting to continue to lie here, I cling to my bed. This morning I am needing more time. And yet this minute Madame is under my bed with her broom. Out from under come a host of missing articles, a single shoe from several pairs, at least; the book I had been planning to get back to. La Foucault on punishment, the execution as an expression of man's attitude toward the body, an interesting subject. I did read the first chapter in which he described a particularly bloody event. A man, I forget who, someone in history, was being drawn and quartered. He told about it in the greatest detail. Frankly, I thought he went on about it, which made me put it down, though I am curious and mean to continue later, not today, but sometime when I'm in the mood.

Now she lines up my shoes against the wall. Why not in the closet, Madame, where they belong? I believe her efficiency is getting the best of her. Far better, to take a few minutes longer. How I should love to be telling her all this! Instead, imagining her response, I say:

"Mieux dans le placard, Madame. Tu ne crois pas?"

"Eh!"

She is so taken aback by my little speech, she hasn't got the drift of it. Very well, I'll say it again!

"Mieux dans le placard, Madame!"

"Si vous me dites ça je vais quitter ce travail!"

There and then, she puts down her broom and marches to the door. All the while, she is expecting me to stop her. But I don't. Why should I? What I really want is that she leave. She pauses at the door. With her best face for looking hurt, she delivers her final parting speech in which she tells me how ungrateful I am. She has always done her best. With her hands in the position of prayer, looking heavenward in the manner that she was taught in convent school, she appeals to God as her true witness, she did her best, she says, and takes herself out of my life once and for all.

How quickly it is accomplished in the mind.

My, she's in a temper today. She is talking about me. Listen to the muttering.

"Comme elle est paresseuse!"

In truth, we have reached a new low in our relations due to my disinclination to leave the bed. She says that I am lazy and she is right. She knows how I've been spending my time lately. Listen to her speak.

"J'ai envie de quitter ce travail."

She too has a desire to get out. As she has earned her familiarity, I allow her to continue.

"Je ne veux pas continuer!"

I think she may quit as I am getting worse. Ever since the cousins came, I am not moved to dress for her or anyone. Today I must dress to go out. But a wardrobe goes unused most of the time. And yet I will not put clothes in camphor as Madame has urged despite the danger of moths which may get the better part of them. There is a moth in the room at this very moment! Do I plan to do anything about it? Not on your life! I would far rather watch him do his work. Let him start on the curtains. He may grow fat with their fabric! You'll not hear me complain about the holes. Madame can do the complaining here. In this manner, she can extend her repertoire. For, in truth, I am growing tired of what she says.

Yes, I've been spending my days in my nightgown and my nights too. When she first came to work for me, I made efforts to hide these little lapses. I kept the door closed. I kept both my doors closed if I lay here and in my shame I made motions at her approach, to indicate activity. This wasn't always easy as she could come upon me from two sides. This room, which is study and bed-room, opens out on the porte d'entrée and the salle à manger. Of course, in the best of all possible worlds, it was meant to be a library. A wall is covered with my books. I could wish there were four such walls and no doors. I could but I won't. Not today. For I will be getting ready to go out, eventually. Not now. Not until later in the day.

As Benjamin and I occupy separate rooms, I put up with the disadvantages. I prefer them to what I would otherwise suffer. I suffered before. To begin with, I worked in the salle à manger and slept in with Benjamin. This was the library then. I used the room, but not as much. I did not feel it to be mine. We did sit in here of an evening, especially in the warmer months. Then, it can be airy enough. While it is downright chilly in winter. The windows do not close right! But nothing is ever fixed around here. What was done was done at the first. But to continue, I had difficulty sleeping, at that time. An ailment afflicted me at night most particularly. When I had the first attack, I thought it was appendicitis. So did Benjamin, who called the ambulance. Fortunately, we stopped its coming in the nick of time. For, as it turned out, my appendix was fine. Perhaps, it is a spastic colon, I said. A cousin of mine had had a similar complaint. But the pains continued to be terrible, not on that night, but another. I was truly afraid; thank God a doctor in the neighborhood agreed to come. He gave me an injection which was marvelous. I wish I could have it now. But he has gone to another city. Was it in Normandy? He did recommend me to an internist with an office on the boulevard Sébastopol, a Dr. Weissman, whose opinion it was that I suffered from a neurotic complaint, comparable to migraine. There was nothing to do for it but relax, he said, which I felt was an impertinence. The more so as, with his hand on my knee, he recommended a nudist colony. He knew one in the south of France, on an island, he said. Such kindness was misplaced, I assured him, and removed his hand from my knee. I had no interest of that kind. "You don't understand," he explained, "I go there with my family. Go there on your own or with your husband." He was a stout little man and I think he meant well, despite the strangeness of his manner.

During the bad periods, which sometimes went on for days, I ate only simple food, leaving out the wine. It did not seem to make me feel better. But still the attacks continued, if in a somewhat milder form, and I became insomniac. As I expected an attack at any time, I could not easily fall asleep. Nor could I just continue to lie in the bed. I got up and walked around. But the walking disturbed the sleeping Benjamin. He is a light sleeper anyhow, and prone to get into a temper when sleep is disturbed. Benjamin has a theory about sleep that I think is rather interesting. It is his idea that the sleep that is undisturbed during certain hours in the night prevents aging. If this is true, it is too bad for me. Because those are precisely the hours when I'm awake. Even without an attack, I often am up and reading and I continue to read far into the night. But it was at that time that I got into such a habit. I started to recline on the daybed in what is now my room. There, I began to read or just think. And I learned to find my insomnia agreeable and did not care about the loss of sleep. As for the attacks, they continued to diminish in their seriousness. They were a part of my life. But once I had begun to spend my nights there, I did not want to give it up. This became a source of difficulty between Benjamin and me. He didn't like it and said that if my attacks were psychological, I could get over it. It was just plain self-indulgence to continue in them. I should learn to take control! This I really could not do though I tried for a time. But each night, the consequence was predictable and I wound up again in the same place. In the end, he got used to it, though it was the finish of easy relations. About which he was even explicit. He gave me fair warning, he said.

There are always drawbacks to one's arrangements in life, and we must suffer inconvenience. Even the richest of men endure a lowering of standards. I pointed this out to Benjamin. He found such an idea unconvincing. He never was able to accept a difficulty. But had to persevere until the problem was overcome. It had been that way for him in his schooling and also in his work. He is a problem solver by nature, which is too bad as I remain the only problem he is unable to solve.

For myself, I had thought about remodeling, to improve my conditions of privacy. Why not do away with the extra door, for example. How expensive can it be? Or if the cost is prohibitive, why not cover it with a curtain, build in another bookcase, perhaps! I could use another bookcase. But I am flexible and if I must endure the situation, I will.

Far better to look out my window than bother my brain. I will now watch the good housewives who go about their morning shopping. There are also the street women below. The present government has been lenient toward them despite a preference of Madame de Gaulle. In any case, her husband is dead and the new minister is rather lenient. . . . The street women are out peddling their wares. It is not too early to begin or too late to continue, for that matter. The streets are never empty of them here. You can identify them this winter by their high-stepping boots. The shoulder-strap bag is also in fashion. They stand in doorways with their coats open to reveal a thigh angled out from a rather deep slit. I remember when the skirts were short. Such a fashion did not make sense in the cold. It is cold now; the wind shakes the windows of this house. In here, one of the windows will not even close. As for going out, I would rather not think of it. Outside, people are hurrying. Only the street women are loitering.

Eye work. . . .When it tires me down below, I look up and watch the smoke curl. I see pigeons drop on ledges where they feed and excrete or I look at my hand, white and blue-veined through thin skin against a sky which is gray. I also have my business in grayness. The ashtray overflows. I light a cigarette. I forget. One is already lit. Now I have two. Je fume, je fume . . . I am a dragoness in my bed. . . . I now think that the bed is a necessary part of my form. That it roots me here and that without it, I would (like smoke) curl upward into the atmosphere.

But wait! Madame speaks again. I must listen to what she says.

"Ce n'est pas une vie, ça."

She speaks as if I am not here in the room. As if because I choose not to move at this particular time, I am incapable of locomotion.

"Elle ne me parle plus!"

She says also that as I do not speak to her now, I will no longer speak.

"Cette dame n'écoute plus."

Further, that I do not listen. Is it a bad thing that I do? As I do not speak to her or get out of my bed now, I am the freer to do what I want, to imagine, perhaps, as writers do, also speculators. I have considered both these professions. I have tried writing and have at one time or another accumulated myriad pages which are scattered now, in boxes and drawers. Some have been thrown out. Thrown out by you, Madame! I have myself discarded pages. That was some time back. I found no story in them, no evidence of consecutive thinking. Neither did I find a character, unless I count myself. There were too many I's in my text. Nowhere to hide my subject, me, on display. Do you buy it? Not a very interesting offer, I'm afraid. Therefore, I conclude that I am better as I am, free of all artifice, if that is possible. Some would say that speech is an effort to entangle, that the effort itself is therefore artifice.

Better to be an imaginer or an imaginator, if you will. While this constitutes no recognized niche, what of that? It is better than what some do! It is for myself, at least, which is more than what cleaning my house is for you, Madame Propre! What if my imaginations are never spoken or numbered on printed pages?

Madame shouts at me now. This is too much! I am not deaf, Madame, nor am I dumb that you should go on this way! She is flinging my things that were on the chair onto the floor. They are not all in need of washing, Madame. But I suppose you don't care. I suppose that you would rather wash than hang them up, Madame, or wait for me to do the hanging up on the back of the nearest chair!

"Ce n'est pas une vie, ça!"

Have you nothing else to say? I believe I have heard enough from my Madame Propre. She'd better watch out, or she'll have her walking papers from me. And I'll give her no reference! What'll she do then? You didn't think of that, Madame, did you?

Her movements become erratic, jerking. I see elbows and knees. She is turning faster and faster, spinning toplike before my bed. Her figure, flat, broad-hipped, broom and duster are about to disappear. She is lost in a whirlwind. You are a whirlwind, Madame. Do you know what I do with you? Only her voice remains now. A voice, I'm afraid, that will haunt me even when I'm gone from here.

It has occurred to me lately that something is wrong with me. Ever since the cousins came, I feel that I am getting worse. I am more easily frightened. When the doorbell rings, I feel that it is bad, never mind the person or the reason. And I am frequently in tears. This, combined with constant shivering, leads me to believe I should seek help or, if this place is bad for me and so too the life that I am leading here, I must make a plan to get out!

I am alone now, save for Madame. Benjamin has been gone for some days. I do not continue to work, not regularly, which may have to do with the fact that I have recently completed a large project. But I think about my ladies. Though thinking about them, I realize, is not enough. The tract, begun before their visit, is done and done well. *The Disease of Modernism* is my translation of the title. Though I'm not clear about the connection between the words, which may be a failure of the work. The thesis may be private, even personal. Of this I can't be sure. The author, one of those professors in the universities, did seem to be rather upset about what he called the state of the humanities. He seemed to feel that as they weren't taught anymore, people would no longer be educated. That is where the disease comes in. As he sees it, the humanities are a sort of antidote. Without them, Western man will gradually sicken and die. Which made me think of my own case. Is it lack of education that lays me flat? I do not think so. My education took place before the revolution of which he speaks. I am no "product of the sixties," as he calls them. Mind you, I was not aware of any revolution in America. I am sure Madame would have spoken of it to me. At least, I think so. But if, in fact, a revolution did occur, it is over now. And as for any cure for the disease of which he speaks, it does not lie in books, which are more than likely a distraction.

But I have forgotten Madame! I remember now that I willed her out of the way. Shall I let her linger there as a fancy merely, not a real person at all? This is not a bad idea, the more so as I remember I plan to go out. . . .

I am seated now at the table having something to eat. I had asked Madame to buy me croissants, an excuse to get her out of my hair. But I enjoy the croissants, all the same. They are the sort with almonds, which I have always liked best. . . . The former owners ate in the kitchen, never in the salle à manger. And yet I find the kitchen impossible as a place to eat. It is small. The tiles are cold underfoot and the walls, while they've been painted over, are now in need of plastering. I let Madame hang the clothes on a drying rack above the partition, which conceals a heating unit. We have central heating here, and a balcony, all the amenities so appreciated here in Paris. I thought we would use the balcony, Benjamin and I, but we never did. I imagined breakfast à deux, a cocktail in the evening, perhaps. Well, it hasn't worked out. . . . Madame now keeps her chamois on the railing. She thinks a great deal of her chamois and never would use rags. Rags, she says, leave streaks. And she is very careful to put them out to air before she goes. Once a chamois dropped from the railing. We now think it happened after she had gone. In the morning, having discovered the loss, she went downstairs in search of it. It didn't seem it could be lost, not to Madame, possessor of all things, queen of the mop and the pail. Nothing would do, though I offered to buy a new one, than for her to stop at each of the neighbor's doors and ask in the most suspicious way: "Excusez-moi, Madame. Voux avez vu par hasard mon torchon? C'était le meilleur, vous savez. Non! Vous êtes sûre? Excusez-moi, alors."

To this day, she shakes her head when she has occasion to eye the railing, as if by her persistence, the missing article might appear.

Madame complains about the noise in the apartment and prefers the curtains closed, even when there is some sun. I have opened them now, which she would not approve. She would say I am at fault, not only for opening the curtains, but for the still larger sin of choosing this apartment, part of an unfortunate history referred to in moments of pique. But would I have known you had I lived elsewhere, Madame? So why then should you complain? For it is very possible that had another woman come here, she would not have found you suitable. . . .Where Madame lives, it isn't noisy. I was to Madame's apartment once. We sat opposite each other sipping Martini, a particularly saccharine aperitif. There was no real conversation such as we have here, which was a little trying, I found. She may have thought it was up to me to begin and I did try. I asked after her husband. She said he wasn't there. He had gone to see his mother in the south. Had she not thought of going herself, I asked. Not very likely, she did not like it there. And they had never gotten on with her, she said. It was because she was an orphan and did not have a dowry, not a sou. But you earn a living, is that not enough? She shook her head. "Les hommes," she said. But it was his mother she had been speaking about! I asked after the daughter. She had recently married an Algerian, she said, which is probably why she hadn't spoken of her lately. This awful question cast a pall on the conversation, difficult to recover from. I did what I could. I admired her furniture, gleaming 1920s modern. I commented on the brilliance of the finish. This caused her to recover some. I remarked upon the good character of the neighborhood and drew out from her a word or two about the people who lived above and below her. She began to feel better. And I believe that by the time the visit was over, she was satisfied. For I had understood for myself that she was no ordinary person and could not be dismissed, that the care manifested in her furnishings was not, as in mine, a holding action, but the ultimate proof of superiority.

Madame comes into the room. She has recovered from her ill humor of this morning. And now that I am out of my bed, she would like to converse with me.

"Vous avez remarquée qu'il y avait un incident dans le Suez." The Jews have struck out at the Arabs again, arousing her sympathies. The Jews are hateful here in the Marais, but the Algerians are loathed by Madame, the more so since her own daughter is mismatched with them. When she can, she whets her appetite for revenge on what is happening.

"Ce n'est pas vrai."

I would say more to her to invite some further disquisition on the cleverness of Moshe Dayan. But as I must be going, I will offer to buy off this thwarted animus with a bevy of detergents. I ask her if she has need of something as I will be going out in half an hour.

"On a besoin encore de lessive," she lets me know. Madame is doing the washing today. In the sink are the very articles she cursed me for while cleaning my room.

But now I see the earlier incident is forgotten, as the Arabs continue to be on her mind.

"Quand je vais mourir, je travaillerai pour le bon dieu!" I've heard this before. When she remembers the work that she does and that it will always be there to do, she refers to the domestic work that one day she'll do for God, his laundry, I suppose.

But I must think of where I go, today. I am going to Gallimard, world-famous publisher of Proust and Gide. It is for them that I do my translations. They know that I am fast. They think I am remarkable though they do not pay me what I deserve. In New York, I would be living high on what I do, not only in fantasy! But not with Gallimard. Never mind. So long as it gets me out. For I begin to think that I am kept here. It is strange. I sit here in my chair and think that I am unable to leave. That the very services I adore are a sop or a mollifier, an elaborate deception, perhaps. It is then I think that no matter how cold it is outside, I must go out. I must be mad! As no one keeps me, it is I who keep myself. I can do what I want, even here, where these very rooms become as chambers of my mind, losing their particularity, if I let them. I do not always let them but look upon them as not mine, faulty. I think of the spaces between the floorboards, the narrow entryway or how the glass shakes in the window frames on days like these, not to mention the doors. Or, I think up an antidote, more work, for example, activity, reducing the time on the bed. I could do it. I could set about to improve my Spanish, for example, broadening my line. I could take a lover. Many have. I am not really so old and unattractive as I pretend!

Walking away from the grander sections of Paris to where arcades connect streets, there is a city within the city, where commerce is transacted. There, I have seen hags for sale, even children, schoolgirls, housewives, prosperous ones, dark ladies of mysterious address who arrive in cabs. Men watch, single out their pleasure and move on. I too could find or be found.

I used to look for a man that I might like, I never saw him. Sometimes, in the distance, I would see a man who might be for me. But when I got closer, there was something which marred, a look round the eyes, or a mouth which threatened difficulty or ears which were not flat against the skull. And if the fault did not lie in the man, it lay in me.

"Je vais partir, Madame!"

I say this by way of forcing myself from the chair.

"A tout à l'heure, Madame!"

But will I see her later? I forget. She goes to the wholesaler down the street this afternoon. One wouldn't have thought there was time in her life for other jobs, but Madame has surprised me.

It was by accident that I found out that she had another client. A month back, no more, I asked a favor of her. I try not to ask too many favors of Madame. But that time, she left me no room. My bedspread was in need of cleaning. Normally, she takes it at the end of winter. But the spread was more than usually soiled, even for me. I had not been feeling well during that period. She had brought me my coffee in bed. As luck would have it, I spilled some while reaching to the night table for my glasses, a pointless accident. I was annoyed and wanted the evidence out. Madame would have waited. She said it was not as dirty as all that! She has her little economies, I have noticed. But in this instance, I could not respect them. I insisted that she take it to the cleaners. She shook her head no. What's more she blushed as if exposed to me. This is not like you, Madame! I remarked. Just what was her difficulty? She would not answer. I asked her again, continuing to hold my ground. Very reluctantly, she answered me.

"Je ne peux pas," she said. "Je travaille ailleurs le mardi." That Madame had been at great pains to keep this information from me was perfectly apparent. She was filled with a sense of her culpability. Not that she didn't have the right to hold another job. She did. But rather because she did not wish that I know of her involvement with other lives, as if, by example, she gives a permission to me.

But not satisfied with the incompleteness of her answer, I was determined to find out more. The very next morning, I began to continue my questioning. I asked her what it was that she did where she worked. She did many things, she told me. She was beginning to recover from her initial embarrassment of yesterday. She was now only too willing to answer my questions as if she wanted to let me in on more of her life. I wondered why.

I had to conclude that she saw advantage in letting me know other arenas in which she might take me on, showing me the superiority of her existence. But perhaps I am hard on her. She is after all a simple woman. But she is a woman all the same.

Tell me, I said to her, wanting to draw her out further, tell me all about what you do when you work.

"Je fais tout," she began. At first, it wasn't like that, she said. She only did the cleaning. And I could see for the very first time how it was that Madame had moved in on my life. Then, she told me, she was doing buttons and hems. Soon it was their accounts, and I suppose that before she's done with her other employer, she will do what she does with me, take the work home, take them home too!

As if it weren't bad enough that she held another job, she admitted to holding two.

"Je suis gardienne," she acknowledged, fiercely pleased with herself by now. This caretaking work apparently goes on at home, in her building. There, when lesser mortals have returned home to carefree evenings with their families—for she lives where there are offices —she is able to look after the money.

"Comme ça," she concluded, "je travaille la nuit et le jour." And her face lit up with feelings of near joy!

I found that I resented not only her revelation but also the manner in which it had been made, with no care to what I might feel. After all, it doesn't reflect well on me, her principal employer, that she does outside work! She might have asked for an increase, I thought. I

110

would have gladly come to terms. I offered her an increase there and then and to my astonishment, she refused.

Her manner of refusal was most definite and I thought it represented her sense of that occasion and the pleasure she took in it, refusing me, letting me know that their desire to continue to have her work there was precisely the compensation that she needed. And when I asked her more particularly why not, there came an answer I might have anticipated.

"Ils ont besoin de moi," she said. They had need of her, as do we all, Madame. For that is your genius: that you make our lives seem impossible without your help. And then I realized that I hardly knew how to do anything, anymore. More to the point, I did not feel that I could do anything, a feeling that was familiar, known to me, I suppose, in childhood.

And of these other clients of hers, I wondered, are they so completely in her keep or am I the most extreme of all her cases? I resolved there and then that something must be done about it, and soon!

"Je vous dois cent cinquante francs, Madame Propre."

"Ça fait rien! Vous pouvez me payer la prochaine fois." Such confidence is misplaced, don't you think!

9

Going Out

In the protection of the green door, I look on the street life I am about to enter. Etienne-Marcel crossing Turbigo. Here, in the undersides of Paris, the day grinds itself out, awnings unfurled over bistros. Les Halles behind me is disarmed but not yet defeated, though they say that it will be soon. And that in its place will be a trade center, not a park as we supposed. Cars and trucks are stopping and starting. The stink of the gas fumes comes up at me. I want to go back in, if only to recover from the shock.

I feel odd going out. I am aware of my body, of the parts of my body in motion. It is as if I have to teach myself to go into the world again. Why should it be so difficult? Why should I question if my arms swing with my step or the opposite? Perhaps they do not need to swing at all? Is it because I go to see my publisher today that makes me feel as I do? I have made a special effort to appear well.

I will examine the passersby from where I am, just to be sure of what they do. I am looking at a mother, the one who wears the ratty fur and has blond curly hair at shoulder length. She does not question what she does with her arms as she has a basket to hold and a child, which makes me think that we are meant to be useful and that the concern to appear useful is another sort of question. She knows that she must hold tight to her child or she will lose him and that the weight of her basket must be borne if there's to be food in the house. A husband awaits her, perhaps she has another child as well. Go on your way, Madame. I will await another to come by.

Here's another. This one has no child. With her hands in her pockets, she signals me that her life is her own and she is free. She has been to see a friend. Perhaps, he is her man. Perhaps, she has no man at all. But she has a place to go and she is happy! I also have a place to go. In my satchel, I have the finished pages of the tract which I deliver to my publisher.

There are those who take their body for granted. I do not; mind and body are like Serbs and Croatians, unhappy members of a single state. But perhaps I have posited an ideal condition which may not exist! I only speculate, bound as I am inside my skin. . . . I am waiting in the doorway for the right moment to go. . . . I will go now, clutching this satchel to my chest, breastplate, armor. It is the schoolgirl's way. Therefore, I will transfer it to under my arm, creating a concern which did not exist before. What about this arm which goes unused? Pockets could be useful here. These are mock pockets but perhaps they can be altered. I'll speak to the seamstress tomorrow. Perhaps she could take a piece of the lining from inside the sleeve and form a real pocket by opening up the seam. Come to think of it, she can also redo my hems. Of course, I know how it will be. She will be standing or kneeling with the pins in her mouth. She will say yes Madame or no. But when I get them back again, I'll find she didn't listen to me. I will have to make another trip, possibly two, in order to convince her to make the alterations. She has her ideas about skirt lengths. The person doesn't matter. The person isn't important unless they spend more, come more, talk to her. I know. I see how it is. With a customer she likes, her energy returns, pins fly, and the past is evoked.... We are at the reception of M. le Comte and Madame la Comtesse de la Bigne. The dresses are a triumph. And who is the heroine of the evening? Not la Comtesse. Neither is it her eligible daughter. It is the seamstress herself.... Then will follow the sad story of how the de la Bignes lost all. The sympathy of the seamstress is fully theirs. Whereas I will find that I feel very American, very democratic, even revolutionary. Then will follow visions of a mob which turns against them: "Down with the de la Bignes! Down with the little seamstress too!" Comes the revolution, I will find she won't be necessary. For then there won't be any more "costumes" or "frocks," only uniforms; these, Madame seamstress, will be made out of hemp, crude and ill-fitting affairs. Where will you be then? You with your fine airs and your fancy aristocratic balls! I'll tell you where you will be, that is, if you aren't dead in a ditch with your friends. You'll be amongst a legion of seamstresses, all of them silent save for the cutting sounds they will make, *snit, snit,* and the machines which will be whirring. . . .

It is cold today. See my breath smoke. . . . The smoke is real, though it doesn't seem so. But science is mysterious to me, making discovery possible. I discover what I've forgotten as well as the no longer discoverable. I am like some painted savage, who finds the world mysterious, gods and demons everywhere.

But I should forget resisting joints, the arm that has no function, the process of walking itself. And I must think instead of where I go. I go to Gallimard. . . . Once, in Gassin, in the restaurant on the end, the one that has the pretty blue plates that come from Valleris, not knowing M. Gallimard, I saw him there, corpulent, puffy-eyed, weak in the knees from arthritis and drink. He turned in my direction, letting me see the man in him, irrepressible even in advancing age. And I saw the no-nonsense truth-uncovering look of him, taking me in. No doubt he wondered who I was and why I came to sit there all alone. For Benjamin was not with me at the time. He had flown from Nice back to Spain to trouble-shoot again. There was no point in looking away. I thought, If he were younger, if I were older, if our lives could come together in some way. But it was a long time until I did meet M. Gallimard. How nice it would have been to have those eyes, softer than his judgments surely, deep, providential, on me. His cane was resting at an angle on the back of his chair. That it was plain and yellowing, contrasting with his naturally important looks (he is a man of some position, after all!) seemed touching to me. I started to look at canes, which I had never done before, desiring to purchase one. I asked proprietors in antique shops to show me what they had. I had nothing else to look for. . . . Later I heard from one of the secretaries that he'd been ill. He was in the hospital again though what the problem was she could not say. She was surprised that I should be interested. Was I acquainted with M. Gallimard, she wanted to know. I said that I was not. But all the same I thought that she was curious that a woman while not young should be interested, apparently, in him. Of course, she could not understand the quality of such an interest as I expressed. She assumed that it was sexual.

I am walking today because the metro invariably alarms me. I don't remember the way. Do I transfer at Châtelet? Nor do I like the mechanics of having to make my way down to the platform, which reminds me of a dream of living underground, riding in trains, depending for my life on the vending machines. Putting the franc in, getting back the sandwich or a biscuit which is dry and crumbling in my hands. Looking for the machine that has the newspaper, making a mistake, looking further and finally getting it. Do I have the right change? When I run out, will there be a machine to give me more?

.... In the dream, the platform is empty. There is an odor which is sweet, succulent. I never discover the source. A car pulls into the station. The doors open and I sit down. I am aware of the perfume still in the empty car. I consider my situation. I feel that it is better on the train. The vibrations of the engine cause me to fall into a light sleep. But soon, I am jolted to attention by screeching brakes and an uneasiness returns. Who will be joining me on this train ride? But I do not sustain the uneasiness for long. I am very tired and cannot stay awake. I continue on the train for what seems many hours, stopping and starting, moving between sleep and an anxious waiting. Something is going to happen, I think. Will it happen now? But still the train continues and my fears become somewhat allayed. I begin to read ads.

"Lisez-vous *Paris Match*?" says one grinning female who looks down on me; lipsticked and joyous, she promises some sort of good time.

"Samaritaine, c'est bon pour vous!" A wifely finger points, husband to one side, children to the other, all looking toward a picture of this great store. I turn away from the empty and vacuous faces and look into the blackness outside the train's windows. I look now into the train, at the empty seats. These had earlier on reassured me. But considering my condition, I am now made uneasy again. Will no one then be joining me?

I begin to understand what might have been apparent

earlier on had it not been for the nature of my fears. What awaits me is no more than what I have endured on this train ride, which is that it never ends. . . .

I remember what it was to see Madame again, when she appeared, as usual, at my door. I was overjoyed, ecstatic even. I could not refrain from squeezing her hand. Unused to such attentions, she responded to me with suspicion.

"Qu'est-ce qu'il y a?" she said. But I did not find this annoying. That she was there in my life on any terms, was occasion for rejoicing. But just to calm her, I found a way to explain my behavior. There was something that only she could attend to, that had to be done. And in the end, she was satisfied. . . .

I see that the chestnut vendor is out.

I ask how much and learn that again the price is up. "Mon dieu," I say. I remember when the price was only a franc. As a child in New York, it was a quarter a bag. The smell, a mixture of burning shell and the fruit, tantalizing. I chew each one slowly making a paste before swallowing, prolonging the pleasure.

I used to search the joinings of the furniture for coins so I could buy the fruit. If I did not find any there, I went on to the closets and coat pockets, wherever I could. Allowance was saved for tangibles in the plump red china pig I won at an amusement park, shooting clay pigeons, an activity I did not enjoy or approve really, knowing the birds could be real. I don't know what came over me to do it, the shooting so unpleasant to the ear. To think the money I saved was used to buy glass animals, so fragile and female. But then who did not have their collection of glass animals?

It is better to hug the curb today. The rue de Rivoli is packed. It might be better to cut over to the quais at once. Back of Samaritaine, there's a way. The vendors from North Africa are out as usual. They would sell me coarse bags and belts, blouses in bold colors I never would want to wear. I resent their dark insidious eyes which must remind me of my sex. I know these sensualists of the alleyways only too well. What woman in Paris does not! At night, they lie in wait for the lonely passerby and follow her with promises of Arabian nights. I walk past them as if I do not see them. For soon, if I am lucky, I'll be beyond them. I know one must never reveal in any way a vulnerability or they will be after you. When I first came here, I walked fast, then ran, round corners in the direction of home. I sought protection from the policier on the corner of Cardinal-Lemoine, but found him unwilling to help me. Was it that he could not believe I didn't want to be chased! My pursuer, confident in the chase, waited patiently, on the far corner, denying by his strategy, my reluctance. In the end, I did outrun him, but what if I hadn't!

It was the quiet of the streets that deceived me, and the occasional stroller. I did not notice then what is apparent to me now, that women, day or night, must have a child, a basket, a companion or satchel. By this means, you say what you are and what you are not! Not until old age defines you as death-bound, can you be free of the dangers to your sex! Not until then will I have what men have assumed, which is only a decent margin of safety.

When I am old, I won't be one of those who imagines rapists around corners, though I imagine them now, knowing that the crime might be in my mind, that the hot pursuit and most of all the invasion of privacy are the only crimes that will happen.

A city animal, I am sensitive to my surroundings, the laborers on lunch hour munching tartines, drinking vin ordinaire at one franc eighty centimes. Occasionally, a remark passes but I ignore it and cross the river, where for the time being I'll be done with it.

The vans are out now. The CRS are everywhere. Their bayonets are locked and the crash helmets are on. They are expecting some kind of trouble in the quarter or there is a sensitive trial of a political nature. If I were younger, they would stop me. They might hold me up. I have heard how they put you out of the country if your papers aren't right!

I am getting tired from the walk. If I fell down, would anybody help me? But I want no accidents today so I'll be especially careful. My appointment is at two—or was it earlier? I have the correspondence in my purse.

This urinal on the corner is an unpleasant reminder of our baser natures. They do not hide them here nor do they do what they should about the accumulations from their beloved dogs! How the French adore them, better than their children, I think, taking them for goûters in the cafés. I have seen café au lait given in the name of dog love, and little cakes. How I marvel at their dog love and even envy it, though I should not want the trouble myself. Also, my associations with dogs have not been positive, so I go dogless, into the afternoon. But I have my book, inanimate and resistant, and fingering its pages offers its own sort of compensation. I can release the pages in my hands, letting them flutter down flat or I can feel the cover, if it is well made. Cats are another matter. I had a cat when I first came here who only stayed a little while. She needed to go as she was in heat, which I tried to prevent. In the end, she worked her way out a window in the back of the apartment, a room we have not used since we have been here save to pack with cast-off clothes and the steamer trunks we came with. No wonder I didn't hear her. I went looking for the cat throughout the quarter and found her, eventually, weeks later. Unfortunately, she had gone quite wild. My calls, my offers of kidney, which she had especially liked, did not tempt her to come near me.

"J'ai un rendez-vous avec M. Gallimard."

"Il n'est pas ici le mardi. Vous êtes sûre?"

Not here on Tuesday! Not here, when I have come all this way! I feel sick. The walk, the cold, my head.... What does this mean? I have a letter in my pocketbook. I feel sure she's made a mistake. I should tell her.

"Vous voyez, c'était écrit, ici!"

10

Relations End

It was on the way home from Gallimard, I came to my decision. That I looked forward to seeing the head of the house himself was my stupidity. I had never had occasion to see him before. Nor he me. His not being in the office, I took as a judgment. For, as it turned out, I had gone on the right day, after all. It was an oversight, his receptionist had assured me. We should set up another appointment, she said. But I could see that after all, it wasn't necessary. That I had done the work and I could leave it with her. So, I assured the receptionist that that was unnecessary. There really wasn't any more to say. I would be leaving France anyway, the end of next week. And as I told her of my plan, I knew that it was true. I would leave Paris as I said and I would never come back. But I had yet to tell Benjamin.

I put my cigarette down, no matter it was only begun, the still-fresh aroma of the Gaulois, the wine that I had been drinking, and went into Benjamin's room.

"I'm going away Benjamin."

"What of that," he said, not wishing then to be disturbed.

I, on the other hand, felt the need to set in motion the course of action I had determined for myself, to leave behind me, once and for all, my costly ménage.

"You don't seem to see what I'm getting at! I no longer want to live here. I want to travel and I'm going to travel, on my own!"

"If you want to go away, you can go! You have your own money, why not take it? I won't be standing in your way. I never have! But why are you making more of your going off traveling than is necessary? There'll be an end to your traveling soon enough. And then you'll be back."

"That's just what I don't want. I don't want to have this apartment to come back to. I don't want Madame Propre to continue here. And I don't want you!"

"It's typical of you," he began, "to assume I feel nothing for this place. That is because you have no imagination of my life! My work takes me away. What of that! All men have work which takes them away. You also have your work and it has taken you away, if not from this place, then from me!"

I said nothing. There was nothing at all for me to say to an implication that Benjamin had a right to a wife, to the return he demanded and I refused. I had been discovered idle again and on his time. He had wanted me to do something for him. That was in the morning. I should look to find a missing shirt that he especially wanted to wear. Had Madame done something with it? He had put it in with the dirty shirts a long time ago. It should have been cleaned and in his drawer. I had said that I knew nothing of this shirt that he was speaking about, nothing at all. And that perhaps his question would be better applied to Madame herself. "You know it's not Madame Propre I want to be dealing with about the matter. The responsibility should be yours."

"It should, should it," I countered, "then what do we pay her for?"

"That's what I'd like to know!" said Benjamin. "Because as far as I can tell, as you're not doing anything, you can bloody well take over! At least, make an effort to find the shirt."

"I will not!"

This was a preparation for the scene of the moment, so our tempers were high. The issue between us, this morning it had been the missing shirt, was now coming up again, in another form, of course. I was resisting him, that is all that he would understand, which was going to be a problem, I could see. I sat down on the little straight-backed chair beside the door. Too late, there began between my ears a terrific ache. Should I have started it? Yet, despite the pain, or rather because of it, I had a need for the confrontation that was coming, to make it real. How, otherwise, could I know that I was going and not coming back? Too long was the break between us, inside my head; action and utterance must be one.

I remember long ago when I was studying Shakespeare for the first time, a Mr. Priest drew a diagram with arrows on the blackboard indicating the shape of the classic drama: rising action—conflict—falling action —denouement. Will my life, at last, be expressing its proper form?

Seeing an opportunity in my temporary lack of composure—I was crying by this time—he spun toward me in his swivel seat. I was in his office again, a small-time businessman, perhaps, who was about to be turned down for a loan. My case was surely insignificant. And he was longing to get back to his business, which was important, working out a deal involving several millions of dollars, never mind that the money wasn't his. He drew his importance from it. And for my lack of money, he considered me powerless. This posture had often been assumed in our disagreements, to my disadvantage, and was a source of continual misery.

Before actually getting on with the matter, as if to ensure the advantage that he held, Benjamin put his feet up on the adjoining file cabinet. Higher than it should be to guarantee poise, this wasn't his real office, after all, his new position gave his figure a slightly comic aspect which had the specific advantage of allowing me a little room for recovery. But he was not aware of his effect on me and so clung to the position he was in.

"Look," he said, "I don't know what's come over you. Madame Propre mentioned to me that she thought you were ill. She said you were in bed most of last week. Now what's really the matter? Why don't you tell me? I may be able to help you."

You help me, I thought. Why how ridiculous! There

is no one who is going to help me. But I had to continue with what I planned to be our last confrontation.

"Nothing is the matter with me. I'm not sick. At least, not in any way that you'd understand or Madame. I've been coming to my senses, that's all!" I could see Benjamin struggling to be reasonable. His bankerlike composure was pushed to the limit, the pressure inside him was mounting. Had any business associate so provoked him? I doubted it. For he would not have risen to an executive position with eyes popping, beads of sweat forming on the brow. In truth, he looked more like a revolutionary than a member of an establishment. Reminding himself that it might be I who was put in a corner, Benjamin summoned all his energies to control himself. He would be generous.

"Perhaps what you do need is a change, a rest from this place and from me!"

Does he really care or is he staving off a dismantling which is inconvenient to him? I wish I could tell! I might, after all, be ungenerous to myself. My company was not always disagreeable. There was a time when Benjamin said that he liked my conversation. It was refreshing. For, out in his world, there were only men. And what they had to say was predictable, professional, and dry. How much the dollar can buy or how little. Was the lira falling again? And I have been his little bit of home, his island of America in this otherwise foreign sea. One can grow tired of foreigners. As I am always here, he can take me for himself, the more so when I offer no resistance.

"I'll admit," he continued, "I could not spend my life in this apartment the way you do. Year in and year out, your days are always the same. I have always thought your mode of life a little crazy, but I put up with it. Perhaps I have put up with too much!"

This was more the Benjamin that I was used to, the one, therefore, I could resist!

"Here you go again, going on at me about my life. It's my life, after all, isn't it?"

There is a character in one of Ben Jonson's plays who makes me think of Benjamin. Zeal-of-the-Land-Busy, is what he is called, an appropriate name. Like Benjamin, he bothers people with what he thinks they should or should not do. He is not content with his own life. And why should he be? He's a puritan, an object of satire. He's very funny, in fact. But I suppose the humor in that case depends upon our being at a distance, in the audience. Exaggeration is also an element. No wig or black frock can help me here!

But Benjamin is now ready to answer me.

"But why think in ultimate terms?"

So he's understood me at last.

"I like to travel myself. But one is better with a base. You have been a base for me."

Very quietly, but loud enough that he can hear, I answer once and for all.

"I don't think so!"

With quick movements which reveal the disturbance, he begins to put his papers away. It is something to do. But certain papers fall on the floor. Others behind the desk. Could I ever have thought to affect him so! ... I am moved to think of when I first knew Benjamin, so moral, so stern, so upright in the blue suit we bought together in J. Press, the suit he met my mother in, the one that helped convince me to marry him though I knew I mustn't, that it was a mistake of the most terrible kind, that in the end, his high moral sense could turn against me. The end has been too long in coming. We have battled for a terrain that neither of us really desired. We continue to do battle now or, rather, we begin.

I tried to remain detached. It would be too like me to become involved. This susceptibility had kept me his. I couldn't understand that an actual physical dismantling wasn't necessary, that Madame Propre and Benjamin might continue there even after I was gone. That, in fact, there were advantages to be gotten out of the outward forms remaining as he proposed.

"You can have everything," I said. Were they not mine to give by virtue of the attachment? I never thought of them as his before, not the hutch I found down in Les Halles at a great sale there, or the coffers I purchased from the previous owners, not the desk which was a bargain in some old junk shop, not anything. For it was my effort which had put them in the house. These were to me surely like familiar objects to the blind. I knew I was in my space because of them.

"Don't speak to me of your things. They're not yours to give me," said Benjamin. "Have I not sat here on these chairs and eaten off the tables. I am used to them. They are all mine. You give me nothing!"

I felt then as if everything was taken from me. I

couldn't give him anything, not these things which were no longer mine to give. They were never mine if they were his!

"Anyhow," continued Benjamin, after the silence had passed, "I don't believe in your plan. You'll never go anywhere, not unless I take you, you don't have the guts to make a change! I bet you didn't do a thing today or yesterday. And what about last week!"

"You mean you think I can't do it."

"That's the crux of it."

Who can ever know how the idea of a person held by another person, a husband, a mother, a father, and even a maid can assault, do damage, and capture!

Looking like the oracle, he made his ultimate pronouncement:

"You won't last. You're incapable."

And I felt myself go numb with fear. Could he have been right? Was it possible that I, who clung to the poor thing which was my life, could begin again, change, become some other unanticipated person? But, thought I, enough of this crucifying self-doubt. And I felt welling up in me, perhaps for the very first time, a passion which would take me out of his life and beyond, a desire to confound this most critical of husbands. It is at least a beginning, I thought, and I got myself out of the chair.

"I'm going," I said. "I'll be out of here by tomorrow. Stay if you must, though it hadn't occurred to me that you would want to."

"You flatter yourself," said Benjamin, "that I would be going too. It's this that I want!" And he looked round him at all he would possess. It amounted to a considerable property of chairs and tables, an old armoire or cupboard turned record cabinet. My eyes followed his and seeing his need of things, I was myself released.

"Have it all," I said, as I got up to go. But it would have been too easy just to walk out. He did not want to let me go.

"Well, you let me tell you a thing or two!" said Benjamin. I moved toward the door to indicate my impatience for our little scene to be over. I could feel myself becoming quite tired from it. And I was longing for the time of my recovery when I would be traveling far away from where I'd been.

Benjamin's eyes were suddenly ablaze, he wanted to rivet me there. And if he could not, he was going to have his say.

"If you are going, and I don't for a minute believe that you are, it will be a relief to me. You have been nothing but a stone around my neck. The very idea of you is oppression to me. Do you hear me! To me you are a parasite and a slattern! I have many times wished that you were dead!"

"And do you imagine that I didn't feel it?" I answered him back. "Whether I actually knew the content of what you felt is not important, I could feel it! Why else would I have felt the way I did!" I wondered if I could bear to hear any more, whether, if I stayed there, I wouldn't simply break and crumble into inanimate despair, catatonia, a fantasy of mine. Did I exaggerate? But I tell myself that it is almost all over and that whatever I am suffering now, there will be an end to it.

"To put it bluntly, you're not what I was after in a wife!"

Did you ever let me think that I was?

"I say nothing about your not becoming a mother!"

Who's to say it's my fault? When I thought of seeing a specialist, he said no.

"I let you live as you please, despite the way I felt."

As if there could have been an alternative, so long as we stayed in a marriage. I could not be beaten into a shape to be pleasing, how could I?

"And I paid all the bills."

I suppose he would have preferred that I pay them!

"My demands are few. And what do you give me in return? You tell me you are leaving. And what is worse, that I should leave the apartment and give up the maid, as if you have the right to upset my life. *My life!* Well, let me tell you this. I won't have it! Do you hear me? Leave if you are leaving. Go out the door. And the sooner the better, for all I'll care. But don't for a minute expect me to alter my living arrangements or to believe in what you do. One day you'll be back here. And you'll come on your hands and knees. One day very soon. Perhaps, it will be in a month. Perhaps, it will be in a year. But when you do get here, Madame Propre will let you in. And you'll be grateful to her and to me. You're nothing if you're not my wife!"

I am nothing if I am! Is it over then? I think not yet. Something has been held in reserve. As if to prepare himself, Benjamin gets out of his chair, walks about, picks up what few papers have fallen, and sits down again, feet up as before, not altering in the slightest his position.

"Madame Propre tells me you've had a visitor, a man."

I should have known he'd find an outside cause for what I do. Is it not enough I go away because I'm unhappy here? Such a reason it would seem is unacceptable to Benjamin. Though, upon reflection, I could concede him a point. If I had withstood this life so long, why was I going? Why then? The answer may have been in the fact of my aging. I have thought about it. Enough time had passed to watch it happen. To have waited longer would have been to risk never leaving, the idea of which, and the misery it implied, was sufficient to summon all my energies. I am summoning them now.

"It is so."

"I suppose that you are going off with him!"

I should have known he'd think of my visitor, a man past involving himself with another woman except as a friend.

"I didn't think you capable of taking a lover!"

Does he contradict himself? On the one hand, I am leaving because of a lover, on the other, I'm incapable of having one.

"And that you bring him here, have you no shame? Did you never once think of me!"

He does give me credit for a lot. And this, the consequence of a single visit from a man who is of an age to have been my father!

"You're surprised that I have such information. Admit it! You didn't think your precious maid was my informer!"

Madame Propre, if this is true, you let me down. That you are what you are in my life I have accepted. I have let you needle me, I have let you carry on. I have allowed you full sway. But that you talk of me to Benjamin is too much! Never mind what you say. And that you are grossly mistaken in what you suppose. Do you proceed from jealousy to become my betrayer? But perhaps I allow myself to be taken in by him and you have said nothing at all!

"Madame Propre tells me more than you think!"

How pleased he is with himself, to have thought of a ploy. For I cannot yet think it is the truth. And yet what could she have told him? What has there ever been to tell! Though come to think of it, I wish there had been. It would serve him right! And Madame too!

"The man who came here was my employer."

"A likely story!"

"You don't believe me?"

"Why should I believe you? What do you take me for, a fool?"

So it comes to this! Is there no other construction in such a case? And yet, what is the harm in it? Gallimard might have been my lover. It is possible. It is not as if I never wished to have a lover. And he did come to see me! If not the same day, then soon after. This, after the extreme nervousness about going to meet him, and his not being there, the receptionist telling him the next day that I was leaving. He had come to bring my check. He said quite frankly he was curious as to who had been the translator. That he had taken this opportunity to come and meet me personally. I had asked if he would take tea or coffee. I could pour him a drink, I said. No, he answered. That wasn't necessary. He wouldn't stay long. His man was waiting downstairs. But he would sit down, if he might. Of course, I said. Why not sit here, and I pointed to the comfortable chair. I thought it so kind of him to come here. I did want to meet him, I said. And that he wanted to meet me was very generous. "Why generous?" is what he said. "I always make a point of meeting the people who work for me at some point. The fact of your leaving next week made it reasonable for me to come." My heart was pounding with excitement. It was like being in a play, only for once, it was myself who had the lead, not someone else I'd come to see. My only misery was that he would leave. It was so nice to have a visitor. His eyes settled on my face and I understood that there would be no use in hiding myself. And for once, I didn't want to.

"Tell me," he said, "what is it that brought you to Paris to become a translator for Gallimard?"

"My husband came here for business reasons. I had no work. Translation seemed a way of using what I had and filling up the empty places."

I felt rather pleased with my explanation, but I could tell that he found it wanting. I think he would rather I had come to Paris independent of any man, unless it was himself who was my lover. And yet, the atmosphere wasn't sexual. Rather, he seemed to look upon me as a character with a story, a story which promised more by the looks of the principal character.

"I have a feeling," he said, "that you may have another career inside you. That you will not remain in translation. Do you mind my speaking to you this way? Say so if you do and I will stop."

"No. I don't mind. I find it a relief."

"A relief. Why? Are you not used to speaking?"

"Frankly, I'm not. I'm often alone."

"And your husband!"

"I am leaving him. I decided to leave when I came to see you. Somehow your not being there was a help."

"And here I was feeling sorry that I missed the appointment. I see I should be glad."

I felt in Gallimard's presence a compatibility I never would have anticipated. He did not try to make me feel less! He was interested.

"I said before that I thought you had another career inside you, can you think what it is you might do?"

I was hard put to answer him. For I had now no clear idea in my own mind of what I might be doing.

"I have sometimes wanted to write," I offered.

"Who of us who has a mind has not," said Gallimard. "Though I am not sure that writing isn't what people do when there's nothing else!"

I thought I knew what he meant. Writing, like dreaming and thinking, even speculating, is what occurs in the absence of an action. It requires that you be sedentary, that you exempt yourself from being in the world, for example, which is why traveling offered more of an answer to me ultimately than writing. Writing was something to think about doing. And it came to me that what I really wanted was to be in motion, to escape forever the feeling of stasis.

"I am going to travel," I said.

"That's interesting. Do you know where you'll be going?" And interestingly enough, I did.

"I'd like to go to ruins, to great monuments, not as a tourist goes, not in the season. I want to go in the spirit of a pilgrim. I want to be able to think about what I see."

"You interest me," said Gallimard. "I will enjoy thinking of you out there, a woman, going on her way, alone, without children. Do you never think about men?"

"I have thought about you," I said. "Do you remember having seen me before? Don't you think I look familiar?"

"Yes, now you mention it, haven't I seen you in Gassin?"

I was delighted that he should remember having seen me there.

"That's right. I have gone every summer. But I saw you in the restaurant, over on the end. You were with a large party. Were they your family?"

"Probably. But I can't know since I am not aware of exactly which time you saw me. I go there often, you know."

But I could tell that he was pleased.

We had come to the end of our conversation. What more was there to be said? I knew he would be going. I could not stop him. It was going to happen.

"I like you, you know. But I am an old man, I must be

going. You can write to me if you want to. I would like very much to hear from you."

As he got out of the chair, I could see he had difficulty. He wasn't well. I moved as if to help him, how tender were my feelings toward this man I scarcely knew, but he signaled me to remain in my chair.

"I can manage, you know. Though I'm not what I was in the old days," and he chuckled. His impish look suggested adventures which despite his family, I was sure he must have had. I did hand him his cane, for which he thanked me. It had been resting on the back of the little side chair. And I got him his coat, feeling that it was good to care for this older man if only in these restricted ways. After he had left, I ran to the window to have a last look at him as he went into his car. Though he walked with difficulty and had to rely upon his cane, his gait, the stiffness of his legs and shoulders, expressed a certain pride. His driver opened the door and he was gone. I remembered that at the door, for I did see him out, he had kissed me on the forehead, an appropriate gesture for this encounter.

"So," said Benjamin, "I have been undone by an old man. Madame Propre did say that he was old enough to be your father."

"I wish he had been."

Not choosing to respond to what I had said, he went on.

"Well, if you haven't been in the sack, it's only a matter of time."

My silence before this accusation was disconcerting.

But why should I have answered him? He could have it his own way, if that is what he wanted.

"You are a woman, after all!"

I should have thought he'd said enough. But no. He had to go on with it.

"I always thought that what you needed was a father. Perhaps it's unfortunate I didn't fancy the role. I wanted a grown-up for a wife!"

In these words was truth, of a kind. But the overwhelming truth was the pain that he was in. This sign of weakening before me was moving in Benjamin. He had been too strong, too right for my taste, it turned out. Feeling his vulnerability, I questioned if there might have been a future. But it was not in my interest then to entertain the possibility. I had made up my mind. To go back on what I had set out to do would be to fail, to sink back into the morass of what had been my life. In the morning, I would be going. I said good-night.

But Benjamin did not want to allow me to go sleep, his energy was high. He would talk to me, do anything to keep me there.

"You think you can leave just like that!"

I was determined to have an end of it. I could not listen anymore nor could I suffer the pain. I pushed my way past him to my door. He tried to grab the handle first but wasn't quick enough. I could move fairly swiftly when I wanted to. And once I was safe in my room, I secured the lock and I could feel that the victory was mine. I had done it. I had called our relationship quits. For a while, he pounded at my door and called me

names, "parasite," "slattern," "whore," but he did not go
on with it for long.

I was upset as much by Madame Propre as by Benjamin, that she might have been in his pocket. But as I
was exhausted, I could no longer think about it or do
more. I had a restless night and an awful dream.

11

Ordeal

Cold water. Behind me the rocky shores I leave. Under my arm an infant. Is the infant yet to be born or has she just been through the ordeal of birth? And I, for reasons unrevealed to me, am to be in charge of her deliverance.

Over my head, the ravens were flying, land birds, large wingspan, black, black as the blackest part of the sky, quarrelsome, noisy. Hope and fear were in me in equal measure. I learned the rhythm of the waves, rising on the crest, descending again. Still, the sea was devious. For from time to time would swell up an enormous wave which seemed as it approached me to lay the sea flat. I knew with a sure instinct that I must go below these waters so as not to be caught up and dragged along to my undoing. There was a risk for me yes.

There was a greater risk for my charge. Still, not to go under was certain death and so at the base of the rising wave, late, late in its approach, I dove under and down, deep, holding fast. She bore up, I thought, sputtering some, opening eyes which were as slits, sightless, and closing them again. Did I imagine the raised lids and the sputtering, wishing them as signs? I might have and so looked again. But there was no confirmation to be had.

From time to time, I'd lose track of the ravens and despair. But I went on, for to stop was to go willingly with death and I would not. The sky was dark, heavy with bilious purple and magenta. Then would come an opening or crack of light and blue only to be covered over again as before. To continue was worse, to hope in the light, in the appearance of my guides, quarrelsome, noisy, unaware of my need of them. Intermittently, there would come over me a desire, stronger than before, to sink and not to rise again. Were I unburdened ... if I did not feel the weight of this being, hardly female, not yet alive or only just. . . . Endless journeying, the same, save for the signs, mysterious and deceiving.

But there, coming fast upon me, was a parting of the skies. And the bilious purple and magenta were behind me. And I had a vision of the land I was coming toward, low, flat, treeless. But it was not over. And so I held tight lest I lose her at the last. Carefully, I adjusted her weight on my arm, heavy, sore, but this I did not know before, pushing the head high. And so at last we came onto the shore, exhausted and relieved.

12

Au Revoir Madame

I did leave in the morning as I had said. Benjamin was already out of the house, so we had no further words. Madame, coming in as usual at her regular time, was amazed, caught out, to discover a departure in motion.

"Vous allez quelque part?" she asked.

I told her that I was on my way out as she could see. My bags had been packed the night before. There was little for me to do, therefore. There were certain papers that I was looking for. And then I said my good-bye. I would not be back for some time, I said. I would, in short, be gone indefinitely. She wanted to know if something had happened. I said no. Was it something she had done? She hoped not. She had always done her best to please. I knew that, I said.

"C'est le monsieur, alors!"

I said, not really. It wasn't Benjamin that was the

cause. But she wouldn't believe me. My face was puffy. I looked as if I had been crying. But to tell her would be a gift I didn't want to give her, the more so as she would continue to work for Benjamin. She began to cry as I made ready to go. That it actually caused her pain made me soften a little. We embraced. I assured her there was a place still. My husband would be needing her. Come as usual.

Just as I was about to get into the taxi, Madame Propre appeared behind the balustrade, shaking the chamois out, which was her signal, her flag. I made the taxi wait while I said my private good-bye. . . . I will miss you Madame, more than you know. Here, in a city which continued to make of me an outsider, you with your banter, your particular form of abuse, did take me in. I was your bad child in the years we were together. And, I believe, in your own way, you loved me. Your speaking with Benjamin, your willingness to listen to him, was a small betrayal in the light of our larger history. But why are you outside now, Madame? I thought we had said our good-byes, your red eyes, your scarlet cheeks, the tiny network of veins which no rouge could ever cover, moving outward across your face to the hairline and neck; these were testimony enough. I felt your tears on my cheeks, this, despite your betrayals, which I now forgive you. Though even as we said our good-byes, I spied your shoes under the hutch. You were then in your scuffs. You know I like them put away! But I will reproach you no longer, Madame; as far as you were concerned, you did your best.

"Ne pleurez pas, Madame. C'est pas aussi triste que

ça. Je rentre. Bien sûr, je rentre." She, like a child in my arms, did not really believe me but took the comfort I offered her. She had said other good-byes in her lifetime when she had left the convent school. Did she ever see the good sisters again? She didn't. Life is painful, is it not! We have no choice but to accept it. She will miss me, to be sure. But there is an end to all things. There'll be an end to the messes I make, Madame, think of that!

I will say good-bye to you now, Madame Propre, and I wave. But I do not think that she has seen me. There are so many people on the street. But getting into the cab, I think perhaps she may have seen me after all. For I see her wave her chamois most tenaciously. I will think about you where I go, Madame. I will think upon the snail curling inward in its shell.

No more the raps upon my door which are sometimes resented, sometimes prayed for, no more the conversations over coffee which your hand continually poured. Your service, which was so exquisitely needed in my life, your absence, which was an agony, will no longer be a fact.

I will read Eastern philosophy. I will think about religion and the sea. I will think about me. And as for the service you rendered me, Madame. I can get it in hotels at a more convenient rate.

13

Cher M. Gallimard

You will see by the postmark that I am presently in Cornwall. The season is over. I am one of three paying guests. They call us that here, where my down-at-the-heels hosts surreptitiously engage in innkeeping. Besides me, there are two men, thin, careful in their appearance. Brothers? Perhaps. Lovers, more likely. This is not a family place. I see no children here. I doubt they would ever be welcome. Neither do I see husband and wife. Perhaps the married couples have come and gone with the season. And I have no real sense of what the place is like, save that it is damp within these walls.

I know that this was a gentleman's house. My room overlooks the formal gardens which, while sparsely planted now, have in them some very fine roses. They are in bloom now. There are grazing lands attached to the house. And there are no other houses in sight, only woods and, beyond me, the sea.

The proprietress does her own serving here. They say she is a painter but I haven't seen the paintings. There is something about her, an intelligence in the eyes, that suggests that she has done other work. In the winter, when the guests are gone, perhaps she will set up an easel and transform this grayness with her art. But right now, I see only walls of granite blocks and they are free of any decoration.

Mrs. James is plain and forthright. She doesn't pretend to what she is not, which makes dealing with her easy. There is never a confusion about the bill. If I am not at lunch, it is all right. She does not choose to speak about it. I assume it is the same with the others.

I smile at my fellow guests and they at me. It is understood that we will not strike up conversations. We do not come here for sociability. It is not like the bigger hotels and guesthouses down in Penzance where fraternization is common. I have had enough of fraternization and now enjoy only those hotels where I can be left to myself.

You will no doubt think it odd in me. But I have tired of the human community and prefer my own company to any conversation no matter how trivial. This has not always been the case. I did make an effort. I bought a piece of property, though I no longer choose to spend time there. I thought of it as a place to go on holidays when I might want something of a home. I made an arrangement with a nearby farmer who, for the use of

146

the fields, looks after the place. I told him he may harvest the vineyard in exchange for table wine when I am there. But I begin to think he made the better of the deal. The people in the village were not friendly. They did not understand why I should be there, a foreigner, a woman without family. When I went into the village, they weren't friendly. They did not like it, my owning property. I hired a woman as a maid of all work but she came only once. She said it wasn't comfortable in my house. I don't know what she could have meant. I did everything I could to make a home. It was a distraction for me. But maybe she was right and I had not done enough! To collect furnishings is not sufficient to make another person feel comfortable. I did not feel comfortable myself!

I will have to go to Dijon when I leave here. There are matters to settle about the house. I may put it on the market. I'll make up my mind when I am there. I should perhaps give it another chance. It is possible I might like it better. Often, when I've had occasion to go through that part of France on my way to some other place, I think of stopping but I never do. The train continues on and I am relieved. . . . I am a little afraid of what I may find when I get there. Despite the excellent character of my caretaker, there have been occasional incidents of breaking in, transients, young people, mostly. I understand that it is happening everywhere. But I find it very distressing to think of strangers in my house. What if they came when I was there?

I have given up work. I no longer translate. I travel

instead. I live in strange cities. I winter in Venice, in Budapest, in Vienna and Rome. I stand alone in the Piazza San Marco. I feel the wind go through me in the Colosseum when no sensible Roman would be there, much less an American like me, a traveler, a witness to the passing of time, a lover of monuments. You said you saw another career for me than that of a translator. Did you think of this for me? Please answer if you have time.

I pass many hours in the cafés of cities. I watch the regulars who frequent the cafés, the lovers, the workers, the lonely men and women with their dogs. I find that I no longer desire to learn their language, preferring to remain the tourist. I sit behind my book and let their talk flow over me, discovering cadences unencumbered by meaning, habit, association. I drift off . . . a picture forms.

I am a child. I am small, very small. I stand, hidden I think, behind a door, making faces, thumbing my nose. I am in my old kitchen. We also had tiles on the floor and I am barefoot. I am spoken to about putting on slippers, perhaps. I don't listen. But such revenge is short-lived. It is the all-powerful parent who sees behind the door. He takes my arm, digging his fingers into my flesh. As I have thin skin, he has left a mark. Not a happy picture.

I am glad to be pulled back by the café door which has opened and closes again. A man steps out onto the street. I watch him stiffen to the cold, raise his collar protectively and walk on. I return to my book. So the afternoon goes.

148

I am never in Paris. I associate Paris with the unfortunate arrangements of my former life and I am better elsewhere, anywhere, even in America where the present is everywhere and the past hard to find, where the common landmark is mysteriously not there, where change is assimilated into the pattern of a day, where the ball and chain swing and one is never surprised by the destruction. Yes. Even that volatile landscape would be better for me than the city of an unfortunate marriage.

And in the summer, I seek out those empty beaches of my childhood. I am here now. I have come down to the beach for the afternoon. The cold water and the bitter wind that sweeps through these parts as the season draws to a close pleases me. I leave my sandals and wrap on the rocks and walk down to the water's edge. Once, I walked barefoot in these months but can no longer. One must give time to making one's flesh into leather. One must suffer the stones till they no longer make an effect. I haven't the time, but enjoy these hours still on sand and flat rock. Unshod, I walk into the sea hitching up my skirt and wait for the numbness to deaden the sting of the cold water. Now, it is easier.

I often think it strange that I go no farther, not even when the water is warm. Once, I was a swimmer. I learned to swim alongside the dinghy that bore my name, the *Anna Spring.* As the boat moved along, I would go through my strokes. It was a neighbor who came with me. He had the time. His own children were grown. I thought he had no other work than to watch me swim. Growing stronger, I swam out alone to where the fishermen strung their nets, though I had the imagination of going farther.

Fearless, I put myself in the way of physical danger. There was a time, cher M. Gallimard, I hung from my knees or made myself dizzy, letting the world spin me round till I could stand it no longer. Then I'd shut my eyes till the spinning had stopped and the world came back into focus. Later, I hung from the great rocks of the Maine coast for a photograph, careless of my life. Warnings produced laughter and an invitation to join with me in my flirtation with death. And in my marriage, I dreamed of that time; pictures of danger courted were the pictures of freedom. Pictures taken from outside Ogunquit where summer spun itself out lazily, repetitiously and sometimes dangerously. Now I am free but don't any longer choose to put myself in the way of danger, locating such pictures in time. But perhaps this seems strange to you, M. Gallimard.

My feet form pockets in the sand. The pockets deepen. Taking my feet out from their pockets, I move to one side. The process begins again. I feel undigested shells among coarse granules and the occasional stone. Time has its work to do. The sand will be coarse here awhile yet. Coarse sand marks all the beaches between Penzance and Saint Ives, where I go sometimes to vary a little this eternal scene. If you have never been here, I will tell you that Mount Saint Michael in the distance is homely, nothing to compare to its sibling across the channel. I tire of it, liking only to be reminded of its sweet sister. I went to Mont-Saint-Michel once, after the divorce. I saw the galloping tide rush across the flats making an island of that monument. I had promised myself that return, having missed the tides before, but never went, dependent as I was on the unwilling Benjamin.

I used to think freedom lay in death. Death by drowning or, if one were lucky, death by refusing to live, the stopping of breath, the perfect relaxation of the will. That was the way I might have chosen. But now that I am free of Benjamin and even of my maid, my emptier of wastebaskets and ashtrays, my cleaner of toilet bowls, I no longer need to plot my death. This is my freedom, I discover. I stand by the sea and hear its rhythm, no single beating of the heart, but a rushing sound.

I close my eyes so as not to distract myself with the beauty of this place, the house on the hill where I stay, its garden and farmlands terracing down to the rocks, and the beach which is now behind me. I go on or rather back into pictures, which I can do in this place. I become the child. . . . A child walks along a beach. It is early morning and the tide is out. It will not be in until the afternoon. The girl is alone. A chill breeze catches her wispy hair and you cannot see her face. Her eyes are cast downward. She is looking for treasure along the way, the conch shell, the bit of colored glass dulled and smoothed by the sea, a starfish on the rock, flat out in its final death posture.

Did you ever see a starfish die, M. Gallimard? Here is a picture. . . . I had been walking along the beach most

of the morning. The sun was then directly above me.
My father came onto the beach. He had arrived the
night before. My mother and I had been alone in the
house. Now, he was coming to see me. "Let's take a walk
together, Anna." He would instruct me as we went
along. For he knew something of the natural world. I
did not like his instruction but I was going to force
myself to listen to him. From time to time, I looked
downward and saw in my path seaweed, an old bottle,
bits of wood weathered by the tide. I should have liked
to stop to finger these as they had been newly gathered
by the high waves in the night. But I could not risk
offending him and so I continued. The sun was stronger
now. And still I looked round me as we walked. Just
then, I saw a starfish on a rock caught by the retreating
tide, its points curling heavenward for life. It had no
chance on its own. He, too, was caught by the sight of
the struggling creature. I moved instinctively toward it.
He stopped me, catching hold of my arm, making me
halt there with him. I was going to be instructed, I saw.
We were to wait for the death and return with the specimen. No specimen this to me! It was a poor thing, no
less for being low down on the evolutionary scale. I
resisted him in his desire to bring the dead creature
home. It was his trophy, not mine. "You are a foolish
girl, Anna," he said, "and I am going to cure you of
sentimental notions, once and for all." Against my will, I
waited there for the starfish to die. I should have run off
countless times but was prevented from doing so in the
name of science, in the name of reason. It didn't take

long. Half an hour, perhaps. Specimen and child were marched back to the house; the verdict had been passed. Once again, I had flown in the face of reason and was therefore unteachable.

The child is alone now. She lifts her head. I see her full-faced, oval-faced, small-featured. Her eyes do not see or rather they see inwardly to another country where impressions gather to her. She will not speak of these impressions because they have not been released to her. There isn't language for them. Later, she will try to find the language, but she will fail and so go unknown in the world.

I see her walking to a high point near where the fishermen will secure their dories. She sits down at a secure distance and waits. The fishermen, booted and yellow-slickered in the pink and gray morning, jump from their boats and now push the dories onto their tracks and up to the part of the beach that is nearer to the child. Beads of sweat form rivulets down the backs of the men as they push the boats. Together now. Now they have pushed them up away from where the tide will come later in the day. The baskets of fish are taken out. One of the fishermen waves to the child, he has seen her there before. But, as the work is done, the action of the morning over, Anna is already on her way back to her house where she will join the others and so his gesture has gone unnoticed.

When I am done with this place, I will go to another. Work doesn't attract me anymore. I find I am made uneasy by the idea of work. I realize the evasion inherent in the preoccupation. There has been enough evasion in my life. If I do nothing more than stand here on this beach until the end, it would be better for me than the work I did. I have come to think of my translations as evasions. That is all they were to me. Still another version of a story which doesn't really have to do with me or a study which should never have been remotely my concern. I tried all the forms, all manner of gifts, becoming them without discrimination, following their lines to the end, my own unlived lines.

Now that I no longer work, I can travel or rest or summon my pictures. Pictures interest me more. Now a picture forms. . . . A sudden thunderstorm. Lying under the branches of a large spruce, protected and warm. The rain stops. Suddennesses in weather are common in New England. A boy appears, followed by a band of his companions. Amongst these is a boxer dog, strong-chested, short-legged, saliva coming out of the sides of its mouth. I do not like this animal nor do I like the excitement on the faces of these children.

Only as I stand up and come away from the tree do I see the cause of the excitement. They are in chase of a cat, a yellowing aging tom perched uneasily now in the tree which is next to mine. There is laughter and increased excitement as one of the children, the boy who's been in the lead, steps toward the tree and takes hold of the branch, dirty-faced, scrawny, blond-headed boy. I recognize him now. He's the son of a family in the neighborhood. Timson is his name, Timothy Timson. Even as I stand here, I can't believe what, in fact, he's

154

intent upon doing. The boy takes firm hold of the branch and begins to make it sway, back and forth, gently at first. The cat digs his claws in. The boxer responds with increased barking, putting his front paws to the base of the tree to gain advantage of the tom. To whom does the boxer belong? Why doesn't he claim him! Now the boy begins to shake the branch more vigorously and the boxer readies himself for the catch. The children shout him on and the cat falls, easy prey to the dog.

Not wishing to go far, I was uneasy about travel at first. I bought a ticket for Brittany. The idea of Mont-Saint-Michel, no farther than a day's train ride, a day which put a world between me and my former life, got me through the difficulty of leaving.

I set up in a nearby hotel. The patron and his wife were obliging, moving me to a quieter room at the end of the week as I had asked. The clattering of pots and pans had given me some uneasy hours. But once I was in the other room, I could enjoy the crisp cotton sheets and a pleasant airy view. And I went every day to visit Mont-Saint-Michel growing out of the sea. . . . The flat lands surrounding. I walked up the narrow cobbled street, no tourists to distract me in my out-of-the-season visits. Climbing to the highest point, I could let in the distance, a figure walking, a dog who follows. I watch as they disappear into the end-of-the-world flatness. The sea is coming in . . . miles out, at first, then closer. While it is coming nearer, I imagine myself on the flats, caught up by the galloping tide and carried inward to death, perhaps, and then a new life. Conversion by sea. . . .No more death . . . . No more.

Now, in winter and in summer, I move as I am moved, by a whim, a memory, the desire to see again a monument, a relic, a place. I have my favorites, the island cathedral, the tapestries at Bayeux, the Piazza San Marco, Vézelay. And I like the goings and comings knowing that not far from where I am, there is a house which is waiting for me. If I tire of what I am doing, I can stop. And if the house I have no longer suits, I can find another. Meanwhile, I enjoy the riding in trains, in compartments in trains where I am jostled amongst a worker family. The man takes the bread from his wife. She offers me some, the agreeable stranger. I smile but I refuse the bread. We are each pleased by our part in the encounter. It is hot. We fan ourselves with the paper. Or it is cold and we wrap ourselves tightly in arms or outer things. There is a businessman in the compartment. He looks into my face. It is a long way between Zurich and Milan. He thinks better of it, returning to his newspaper, which he carefully refolds. . . . These acknowledgments are sufficient. I return to my reading or to eyeing the countryside or the industrial undersides of cities and the freight yards that signal their approach.

Channel crossings are also pleasurable. I'll be crossing the Channel soon again. . . . Night crossing . . . I stroll on the deck or watch the stewards cleaning up, so practiced, so indifferent to the passengers who remain awake. I am awake among the sleeping bodies stretched across the leather couches, in chairs; whole families who are returning from holidays, bobbing like corks in a sea of furniture. A child's leg dangles, then an arm. Occasionally, someone awakens, checks his watch; seeing the

hour, he goes back to sleep again. In the difficult crossings, the furniture slides, the glasses tumble and crack
but even then, the passengers sleep on.

I am here on the very beach I dreamed of in my
marriage. No southern beach crowded with sun wor-
shippers and swimmers but a beach empty of tourists.
It is not as I had thought, an invitation to death. I join
the universe again. Far better this than an imagined
love, a shipboard romance, an affair turned sour in a
marriage, and the sense of what is lost that must follow.

My needs are simple. Something warm to drink in the
morning, perhaps a little toast and marmalade to sweet-
en the day, a place to walk, a book to read, nothing
that is taxing, I'm afraid. Essays by Miss McCarthy will
do or Orwell's "Politics and the English Language."
These days, I like the simple sentence best. I am way-
ward enough and desire a contrast for my pleasure.

When my day is done, I like to have a good dinner. I
am particular about what I eat and must always have my
glass of wine. I do not skimp on the wine knowing as I
do the pleasure it brings, the sense of smell indulged in
the bouquet, the first sips suggesting other wines, other
places, and the inevitable lightening of self. That particular form of indulgence has always been sweet to me. I
take my time over the wine list. And if I find it wanting,
I make my displeasure known. As I am a welcome guest
wherever I go, regular in the paying of bills, likely to
return if the service is good, proprietors are only too
happy to accommodate me in my desire.

I need the sea and seek it out by early afternoon. . . . It

is early afternoon. The fishermen are back with the catch. I walk by their boats. I am the tourist. I come to see the washing down of the decks, the hanging out of the nets, the securing of the ropes. They do not pay me much attention as I've become a part of their landscape since I've been here. Once, they started up, looking curiously at me. Not as in the village near Dijon, with hostility. I saw myself as they saw me. A woman in her middle years, hair pulled tightly back from her face, tension round the eyes and mouth which even in the dullest weather evinces a continual suffering from glare, hair that might have been beautiful once, now thinning and lusterless. I make no effort to stop the years. Visitors from time are welcomed by me, the creases on the brow, the chin that is less than firm, aging the release I have sought to be free, to come and go without particular notice.

One pauses, a fisherman, expression intent, fingers stiffened to stop the glare and form a visor. Perhaps I stir a memory in him. Another woman whom I might resemble. A teacher of his, years back. I have about me the look of the schooled woman, the woman who did not breed but made a life of books. Though this fisherman knows nothing of books now, he might once have been curious, and moved perhaps by such a one as I in his long life. He looks at me still, which is his right. I am the stranger, not he. I am the one who has entered his range of vision which more usually goes undisturbed.

We reverse roles. He is now the tourist and I the object of curiosity. The tourist and the voyeur, I often think, have in common a desire to enter other lives, other worlds, a vicariousness of the spirit. Finding in the visual mode a safety to range unimpeded by action and its consequences. So this man is to me now and I to him. I like this figure of the man in the distance. I have noticed him before. And he me. Our eyes meet briefly and slide away. He returns to his work. This much and no more, do we serve each other. I stay awhile. I do not want to miss the sight of brightly decorated boats, masts painted black, the trim, orange and green, red and yellow. Bold colors. I am pleased by such marks of frivolity.

Later, I think to take my rented car on a last tour of a favorite Iron-Age village. It is just above the old tin mine of Ding Dong. I'll cut through the fields taking my own route to that silent and mysterious place from where I will be able to see the shape of the land for miles. I'll see other hills, other remains of villages and the occasional cottage. This is a sparsely populated part of the world. History having gone elsewhere. I'll walk again through the remains of that earlier civilization, make out the shapes of their dwellings, outlines now, thumbnail sketches of a simple life where fifty miles was more than any man might expect to travel in a lifetime. I'll come upon some tangible aspect of a life, an oven, a mill, a bit of crockery lying in a field and take it in. I'll sit for a while on a stone wall, a city wall, serving some farmer now as fencing for cattle. I'll watch the wind moving the grasses and feel it working its way through to me. And then I'll be on my way.

I do not worry about what I do next. I don't require more than the next activity. And if my morning on the beach and my tour of the fishing port tire me, why then,

I'll put off that visit until tomorrow or the day after. There is time. As I am alone, there need be no definite arrangements.

I'll pick up a guide next time I'm in Saint Ives. The sort with train schedules for Britain and the Continent. What's the name of that guide? I've forgotten again. My mind will not hold many names. Still. The man in the bookstore will remember. He very kindly remembers his titles. And I can think about the next journey. I have in mind to visit a city, Vienna, perhaps. I was told I had an uncle in Vienna, though I can't imagine he speaks English. But before I make any definite plans for my winter, I have a mind to wait here another week for your answer. If you are not able to write here directly, you can find me at the Dijon address with which I close this letter.

I hope you are well. I have often thought of our conversation in Paris. That was a long time ago now. Will you remember me? I was once the translator for Gallimard. You came to see me at my apartment and did me the kindness to say I might write to you and that you would answer me.

Sincerely,
Anna Spring
13 rue de Thorigny
52003 Dijon

DEMCO